HEART'S
SURRENDER
FOR PEGGY

BY DOROTHY MARTIN

MOODY PRESS
CHICAGO

Other Books In This Series

A New Life For Peggy
Open Doors For Peggy
More Answers For Peggy
A Mystery Solved For Peggy
Hopes Fulfilled For Peggy

CONTENTS

Fiction - Juvenile

1

Peggy's Problem

THERE WAS AN UNDERCURRENT of restlessness in the library that afternoon which showed itself in the numbers of times chairs were scraped across the floor and feet were shuffled under the tables and bursts of conversation were stifled suddenly. It was hard to tell just what was responsible for the atmosphere. It might have been the crispness of the air coming in through the open windows, or the sight of golden leaves drifting lazily in the wind and then suddenly swooping to the ground, or the anticipation of the football game that evening.

Peggy and Alice had stopped in the library on the way home from school to look for material for a term paper, and now Peggy, looking aimlessly along the shelves for something interesting to read, wondered how long it would be until the first couple was booted out. It didn't take any brains to figure out which one it would be, for the blond with the french twist and silver fingernails had apparently come in with the intention of driving the librarian mad. Miss Johnson had progressed from stern looks at them to an indignant tapping of her pencil on the desk and finally to a severe, "Quiet, please!" but with no success.

Then Peggy half turned to look over her shoulder at Alice and Bob. Bob had followed them into the reference room, and he and Alice were comparing notes on an

7

assignment. A couple of fellows, former friends of Bob's, had stopped at the table, and their audible wisecracks were not being appreciated by the librarian.

The explosion when it came was loud and decisive. Peggy had sat down at the far end of a table and now watched as the blond and her date were told to pack up and leave. Then Miss Johnson headed grimly for Bob and Alice, who looked up at her a little apprehensively.

"This is not a visiting room!" she snapped at them. "Nor is it Grand Central Station, even though you make it sound as though it were. Either stop all your conversation immediately or leave the building."

The other fellows got up and, with a mocking bow, walked nonchalantly off while the librarian continued to look at Bob and Alice. Then Bob, with a grin, whispered loudly, "Okay, we hear you."

For some reason this infuriated her, and with a tight-lipped motion she made it clear that he was to leave at once. With a shrug he bundled his books together and stood up, looking down at Alice.

"Coming?" Peggy saw his lips ask, and Alice nodded. Then she remembered Peggy and looked apologetically down the length of the table at her and back up again at Bob and whispered something to him.

He nodded and looked over at Peggy then, including her in whatever the invitation was, but she shook her head resolutely and tapped the book she had just taken down from the shelf. She had wanted something as a protection for just such a situation as this. She didn't intend to be the third person on a date all the time.

But as Alice stood up, pushed in her chair, and followed Bob, Peggy watched them cross the reference room and go through the reading room to the door. There they stopped and Alice said something to Bob before turning to come back to the desk. Her clear, sweet voice carried easily to Peggy's ears, though she kept her voice low as she said earnestly, "I'm sorry. We really didn't mean to be rude."

She gave the librarian an appealing smile and then, without waiting for an answer, turned and crossed again to where Bob waited.

The glimpse Peggy had of them as Bob pushed open the door with Alice's laughing face turned up toward him made her throat tighten and her heart turn with envy.

She despised herself for being so jealous of Alice — and of other of her friends who dated so effortlessly — but was powerless to stop the longings and envyings that gripped her. Her mind went over the well-worn reasonings she gave herself whenever she thought of the subject. It wasn't that she wanted to go steady, she thought now again. All she wanted was an occasional date, just often enough to reassure herself that she wasn't completely repulsive. There were lots of girls she knew who were no better looking than she, and yet they dated constantly.

And it wasn't as though she wanted a date with just *anyone,* she went on arguing to herself fiercely while her eyes scanned the lines of the book and her hand automatically turned the pages.

"I might as well wish for the moon," she thought, miserably. "Larry never will see me as anyone except Ann's friend. And he probably doesn't think of me *that* much even."

With a sigh, she reached for her purse and stacked up her books as she realized how late it was getting. She'd have to tear to get home in time to help with supper and get ready for the game. Coming down the worn steps of the library, she sniffed appreciatively, taking in all the odors of fall that were so stimulating, and a feeling of exhilaration began to push away the depression that had weighed like a blanket all afternoon. Like a child, she scuffed home through the leaves, her lips quirked in a smile as she remembered how many falls and springs she had walked these streets toward home, often with a problem that had seemed unsolvable. And yet it had always been lifted. Her favorite little chorus hummed its way through her mind and, though the words were not great poetry, the thought and meaning behind them had often brought her out of the dumps to the reminder that she could turn all her problems over to God. So she hummed the melody quietly to herself, fitting in the words.

> Got any rivers you think are uncrossable?
> Got any mountains you can't tunnel through?
> God specializes in things thought impossible,
> And He can do what no other one can do.

She was strolling along, engrossed in her thoughts, until the chiming of the courthouse clock made her practically run the last half block.

By persuading Bill to help with the dishes, she was ready when Ellen's mother honked at seven-thirty. Throwing a hasty good-bye over her shoulder, Peggy escaped before her father could ask if she needed a lift home. It was so humiliating to have to have your father come after you all the time. And it tied you up and prevented your accepting an offer from someone else — if that miracle ever should happen.

The game was heartbreaking, for their team lost because of one misplaced kick. Peggy and Ellen, in the crush that moved from the bleachers toward the gates, were caught up in the chorus of loud and excited indignation that swirled around them. As they pushed along in the mob, Peggy caught sight of Alice, a huge yellow and bronze carnation pinned to her jacket, just as Alice turned in their direction and, seeing them, waved wildly. Then she and Bob began to work in their direction until they were close enough for Alice to call, "A whole bunch of us are going down for a malt and hold a postmortem. Come with."

Peggy started to shake her head, but Bob broke in, "All the gang from church are going. Come on!"

And Ellen said, "Let's go, Peg. I'll have to call my mother from someplace anyhow, and I can do it from there."

"We'll take you home," Bob promised and turned to break a path for them through the crowd.

The place was jammed when they got there, with kids spilling out onto the sidewalk and even sitting along the window ledges. They squeezed in and pushed toward a round table near the back of the room where the bunch from church moved over to make room for them. Peggy's heart flipped as usual at the sight of Larry's friendly grin, and she carefully chose a seat as far from him as possible.

"Where's the younger generation?" she asked then, looking around for Bill and his friends.

"A bunch of them went over to Tom's house. They're too stingy to pay out money, so they go over and sponge off someone's folks," Larry answered.

"I'd do that too if Alice didn't make me bring her in here." Bob gave a mocking sigh and then looked around the table. "What about the rest of you girls? Want me to pay for yours, too? Ann?"

She shook her head and laughed back at him. "Larry's paying for me. What's the use of having a brother if you don't make use of him for something? He can buy mine until he gets enough nerve to ask a girl for a date."

"It's not nerve!" Larry protested. "I'm just waiting for the right one to come along."

"That's no way to do it," Bob advised. "You've got to start looking. Otherwise how will you know when the right one shows up?"

"You mean you're still looking?" Alice pretended to be hurt, and he retorted, "You don't give me a chance."

Peggy sipped her soft drink, letting the conversation flow around her without taking part. Ellen was carrying on animatedly with a couple of girls on the other side of her and Peggy was content just to sit and half listen. She looked up once to find Alice looking at her intently with troubled eyes, and she forced a smile and a flippant, "What's your opinion of librarians?"

Alice groaned. "Don't I have a knack for getting into trouble without even trying? It must be the company I keep," and she smiled up at Bob.

He had been listening in on what Ann and a couple of girls were saying, and it took a moment for him to realize what Alice had said. Then he retorted, "What I like about Alice is her conscience. You know?" he appealed to Peggy. "Every time she does something wrong, she gets this compulsion to confess. And she makes everyone else get the same urge."

The words were teasing, but the expression in his eyes was admiring, and Alice flushed under his look. Then her eyes met Peggy's, and her voice was so low Peggy was sure only she could hear the tremulous, "I've got a lot of confessing to catch up on," before she retorted spiritedly, "I have to have enough conscience for two people when I'm with you."

Bob shot a quick look at Ann, turned red, and protested, "Hey, that's not fair!"

It was Alice who finally broke things up with a glance at her watch and a panicky, "Yipes! I didn't know it was so late. I've got to be home in fifteen minutes. Those are orders from headquarters!"

"Anybody else want a ride? Peggy? Ellen?" Bob asked.

"Sure. Might as well save my mother a trip out," Ellen agreed.

"How about you, Ann?" Bob asked offhandedly as he waved off Peggy's and Ellen's dimes with a, "I'm big-hearted tonight. It's on me." He looked across at Ann and repeated his question. "Is your big brother your guardian tonight, or do you want a ride with us?"

"Thanks, but I'd better go with my guardian," Ann laughed back.

"I'd offer to swap with you, Alice, but I know you'd refuse," Larry said. "Anyway, it sounds to me like Bob is trying to double-date without an extra fellow along. I'd watch him if I were you."

"Okay, so my friendly offers of help are refused," Bob said with a shrug. "So I've got three girls anyway."

As they started for the door, Alice gave another anxious look at her watch, and Peggy heard Bob say in a low voice, "Don't worry, I'll get you in on time."

Peggy, following them to the car and climbing in, marveled at what a change there was in him from a few months ago when rules, to him, were only made to be broken. Last summer he wouldn't have cared if Alice were in on time or not.

"Maybe you'd better drop me off first," Alice suggested. "I don't think I'll make it otherwise."

"It would cut it pretty close if I took the others home first," he agreed, and headed in the direction of her house.

Peggy hadn't talked to Alice about him lately and wondered if they were going steady. They seemed to be, since they went almost everyplace together. Certainly she had noticed that Bob never really dated anyone else. If he wasn't with Alice, he was always with a group, never with one girl alone — just like Larry, one part of her mind said silently. But Alice sometimes went places with Dan, who hovered on the fringe of the group, a dark figure, quick to take offense even when none was meant.

"It's so hard to refuse Dan without hurting his feelings," Alice had explained once to Peggy. "You know how he is."

When Bob got back in the car after taking Alice to the door, he looked over his shoulder at them and asked, "Let's see, who's next? Ellen, I don't know exactly where you live."

She told him, and they drove several blocks in silence. Then Ellen said, "My mother would certainly approve of your driving. She's a crank on the subject. I don't know what kind of promises I'll have to make before she'll let me have the car."

"I learned the hard way," Bob reminded her, and Ellen, with a stricken look in Peggy's direction, said weakly, "Oh, yeah. I forgot."

When they stopped in front of her house, Bob came around to open the door and Ellen got out with a, "Thanks for the ride, Bob. See you, Peg," and loped up the walk.

"Do you want to come up front?" Bob asked, leaning down to peer in at her, and Peggy got out and climbed in beside him without a word. Then, as the car pulled away from the curb and turned in the direction of Pershing Avenue, she said with a stifled sigh, "Alice's folks are stricter than ever with her since — lately." She hoped he wouldn't notice that she had changed the end of her sentence at the last moment.

"They sure are! Especially since last summer," he added feelingly, which was what she had meant. "I always kind of hate to call for her because they look at me as though I were a piece of dirt or something. The funny thing about it," he went on morosely, without giving her a chance to speak, "the funny thing is that they didn't feel that way before I was saved. You know how I was before — kind of dopey and doing nutty things. Then her mother thought I was tops and *wanted* Alice to go out with me. And now —" he stopped and shrugged expressively.

"That's the way her folks are," Peggy sympathized. "They always have been. They don't seem to see how different she is either. Of course, she's always been pretty and everything, but now she's even nicer. We've been friends ever since seventh grade, so I know how swell she is."

"Yeah, Alice is a good kid," he agreed, and again Peggy was puzzled by his abstracted manner. How could any fellow dating Alice be so casual about her, she wondered.

Then with an abrupt change of subject, Bob said, "The Parkers are sure a swell family. I always liked Larry before I was saved, even though I thought he was a nut about religion. I used to feel sorry for him because he was a preacher's kid. But he sure is one swell guy."

"Yes, he is," Peggy answered weakly, not daring to sound too eager but wishing he would say something more about him.

"And his folks are, too," Bob went on. "They've really helped me a lot since last summer. I practically camped on their doorstep at first to be sure I had things straightened out. Mr. Parker explained a lot about the Bible to me that I had never heard of and Mrs. Parker kept shoving food at me." He was silent a moment and then repeated earnestly, "The whole family is swell."

"Yes, they are," Peggy agreed again. Then, realizing they had stopped in her driveway, she said, "Thanks a lot for the lift," and opened the door.

"Wait a minute." Bob jumped out and came around and walked up to the porch with her. He hesitated as though there were something more he wanted to say and then turned away with a, "Well, see you around," and got into his car.

Peggy stood for a moment, watching the lights disappear down the street and then went into the house. It was funny how she had always thought of Bob as being so self-assured. He certainly hadn't been tonight.

Bill looked up at her from a huge sandwich. "Who was that?" he asked curiously.

"Bob," she answered briefly, her mind busy with what now seemed like an odd conversation, though why it was she wasn't sure.

"So!" Bill was exclaiming. "Poaching on your best friend, eh?" And as Peggy looked at him blankly, he added, "Well, I didn't see anyone else left in the car."

"Alice had to rush to get in under the deadline, so Bob took her home first," Peggy explained. Then, realizing the implication of his words, she looked at him crossly.

"Don't be an idiot!" she said witheringly and went upstairs, ignoring his snickers.

2

A Trumpet for Bill

THE GAME THE NEXT FRIDAY was away, and a party that had sort of been planned for young people's had fallen through at the last minute and had been postponed for a couple of weeks. Peggy hadn't been able to settle down to the books stacked on her desk. She wished the party had gone through even if not many could have come. *Anything* would have been better than sitting around the house all evening doing nothing.

The shrill ring of the phone cut across her blue mood, and she tore downstairs calling, "I'll get it!" and grabbed the receiver. After all, you never could tell who might be at the other end of the line.

But the anticipation — useless as she knew it was — drained from her voice at the sound of Ellen's, "Hi, what're you doing?"

"Nothing. Loafing," she answered, which wasn't exactly true, since she'd spent the evening so desperately hoping for something to happen that she almost ached from the sheer effort.

"Well, do you want to do something?" Ellen asked.

"Oh, I guess so. What?"

"Anything you want. Come on over for a while."

"I guess I'd better not. It's getting late."

"It's only eight o'clock," Ellen objected.

"But I'm going to be out late tomorrow baby-sitting. Besides, I'm going to wash my hair."

"I *should* be studying but I can't stand the sight of books. Honestly, when I think of how much school there is left and how sick I am of it already, I could die!" Ellen sighed dismally.

"Cheer up, in about eight weeks comes Christmas vacation."

"Listen to who's trying to cheer me up," Ellen scoffed. "Something wrong?"

"No. I just can't seem to work up enthusiasm for anything," Peggy answered slowly, thinking what an effort it was even to talk to Ellen. "I guess I'm just tired. Think I'll go to bed."

"At eight o'clock! On Friday?"

"I'm beat, Ellen. Maybe I'll see you tomorrow."

"Come over for supper, will you? My mother's going out and we could have pizza or something."

"I'm sitting with the Anderson kids. But maybe you could come over there. I'll ask Mrs. A. about it and let you know. Okay?"

Peggy wandered back upstairs after hanging up the phone, looked with distaste at the chemistry book she had opened just as the phone rang, and shoved it aside. She dug out an old magazine and flipped to the well-thumbed pages of hair styles and decided to try something new. Maybe that's what she needed, she thought restlessly. Something, *anything* so someone would really look at her.

She heard Bill come in as she finished setting her hair and, pulling on a robe, went to the kitchen which was the room he always headed for first when he came in, no matter where he'd been or what time it was.

"Well! Why don't you have a piece of cake?" she asked, as she saw the size of the one he was cutting.

He grinned around at her. "Thanks, I will."

"I think Mother *intended* to have that for dessert tomorrow," Peggy hinted darkly.

"Yeah, I know. But she said to go ahead and have some."

"I'm sure she didn't mean half the cake."

"This isn't half the cake — only half of what's left."

"Let me pour the milk. You'll slop it all over." Peggy reached into the cupboard for glasses.

"Listen, at Uncle Ed's I carried two big full buckets of milk at a time without spilling a drop," he reminded her and tipped the gallon bottle over and began to pour the milk.

"Oh? Then how is it that whenever you try to fill just one small glass the milk runs all over?" Peggy grabbed for a dishrag.

"My hand slipped," he retorted.

They sat down at the table and Peggy asked, "Where were you fellows?"

"Around," he answered, through a mouthful of cake. "At Tom's part of the time. Then we stopped over at Jim's for a while. Dan was there and beat me at pingpong. He's sure sharp —"

"Dan was there? I didn't know he was with you. I thought he was at Alice's. I thought she had a date with him."

"They just went to the drugstore and sat around for a little while, and then he came over to Jim's."

Peggy only half listened, wondering how she could word her next question casually enough not to show too much interest and still get the answer she wanted.

"Was Ann home?" she finally asked.

"I didn't see her. She wasn't in the basement anyway, where we were."

Peggy wondered why it was that brothers were so dense and not able to see what it was a person really wanted to know. She couldn't come right out and ask about Larry, after all!

"Sure wish I was old enough to hold down a job," Bill was saying. "One that really paid something, I mean. I need money."

"Who doesn't?" Peggy snorted. Then she asked, "What's the big push right now?"

"I want to buy a trumpet."

"Oh, Bill! No! You're not planning to start those squawking noises again!"

"What do you mean?" Bill was indignant. "I can play pretty good!"

"That's not the way I remember it," Peggy retorted. "Don't you remember taking lessons the year before we moved here? What were you — fifth grade or so? It was *agony* listening to you. And Mother had to practically beat you over the head even to get you to practice. It was awful!"

"I was just a kid then," Bill protested. "And anyway, I've practiced since then. Uncle Ed had an old trumpet, and I fooled around with it a lot the last couple of years. It wasn't much good, but I got it to work pretty well. I even played in church a couple of times."

"In front of people?" Peggy's voice was anguished.

"Sure in front of people! Another guy and I played duets for the youth group a lot last year."

"I'll bet you sounded neat!"

"Sure we did! Yeah, there might have been a few sour notes, but nobody said anything."

"They were too polite. And, besides, in that little burg they'd probably never heard anyone who could really play — like Larry for instance." Peggy was glad she'd been able to say the name so casually.

"That's why I want a trumpet so I can practice and get to play as good as he does. We might even get good enough to play together."

"You and Larry?" Peggy exclaimed incredulously. "The two of you *together?*"

"No. Four of us guys have got plans."

"Like who?"

"Tom and Jim and Dan and me."

"Oh, no! Now I've heard everything!"

"What's the matter? You don't think we'd be good enough?"

"Well, that's an obvious reason to start with."

"Okay. Name another."

But Peggy, looking at his challenging, good-natured grin as he waited for her answer, couldn't give one. Instead she thought, "I'll just bet it does work out that way for him — just the way everything does. He just stands around, and things just practically fall in his lap." And she couldn't help remembering the verse about all things working together for good to those who loved God. Peggy knew the verse had a deeper meaning than that, but certainly this much was true for Bill. Ever since he had become a Christian so easily and simply, everything had gone well for him.

Now she noticed that Bill's confident grin had been replaced by an expression of embarrassment as he went on haltingly, "We thought it would be a good way to give a testimony. If we're really good enough, when we get older we could even go out on Gospel teams. That was Larry's idea," he added hastily. "He says guys in colleges and Bible schools do that all the time. We figured in three years or so, if we work hard enough, we should be pretty good."

Peggy looked at him thoughtfully. "How much would it cost? A trumpet, I mean."

"About one hundred and fifty dollars. But I figured I could trade in my old one. Uncle Ed said I could have it any time I wanted it. If I trade that in, I might be able to get about thirty dollars on it and I've got some money saved up. I thought if Dad could maybe advance me the rest, I could pay him back a little at a time."

"I could loan you about fifty dollars," Peggy offered. "I saved some of the money from the nursery job last summer."

"That would be swell, Peggy! Thanks a lot. I would like to get one real soon so we could get started."

"Do the other guys have instruments already?"

"Yeah. Tom's got a trombone. He used to take lessons in school, too, when he was a kid, and then he quit. Jim has a trombone too."

"What about Dan? Can his folks afford one?"

"He's got Larry's old trumpet. When Jim and I were first talking about this, Larry offered it to me. But then, when we decided to make it a quartet, I figured Dan would have a harder time swinging one than I would, so Larry sold it to him for about twenty dollars."

"Sold it? Why didn't he just give it to him?"

"You know Dan," Bill shrugged. "He got real mad when Larry offered it to him free and said if he couldn't pay for it he wouldn't take it. So Larry soaked him twenty bucks. Larry says he wonders how the guy ever got saved."

"What did he mean? What does that have to do with it?" Peggy was curious and eager to prolong any conversation that even remotely involved Larry.

"Well," Bill explained, "he says that with salvation a free gift and Dan so afraid someone is feeling sorry for him, he's surprised Dan would be willing to be saved without doing something to earn it. You know how Larry can put things."

"What did Dan say?"

"He got kind of red and stiff at first. Then he said that was different and you couldn't pay God for anything except by giving Him your life. But he wouldn't take Larry's instrument free. You know, Peg, I don't think anyone would ever remember that he was a refugee once if he would only forget it himself once in a while."

"I think he's proud of being different," Peggy sniffed.

"I don't get it. He hates the idea," Bill argued. "He's crazy to be just like the rest of us guys."

"Oh, you'd have to know something about psychology to understand," Peggy replied loftily. Then she added, "Apparently it doesn't bother Alice anymore or she wouldn't go out with him."

"She's sure a dizzy dame," Bill exploded. "She was supposed to have a date with Dan tonight only she forgot, she said, and made one with Bob too."

"I'll bet Dan was mad."

"He was pretty grim for a while. But he got over it. That's what he gets for being dumb enough to want to date her."

"Just wait," Peggy said. "Someday you'll eat those words."

"Not me. I haven't got time or money to waste on some goofy girl."

"Boy! Am I going to remind you of this someday," Peggy jeered.

"Larry and I've got the same idea —"

"You and Larry!" Peggy scoffed. "You mean Larry got the idea, and you copied it."

"Anyway," Bill ignored the interruption, "Larry says the best thing is to be friendly to everyone. Date somebody, sure, but not pick out any one girl to go steady with. He can't get Bob to see it though. I guess he's too far gone on Alice."

When Alice called the next day, her voice was full of exclamation points as usual as she poured out her story of completely forgetting about Dan.

"Honestly, Peggy, it never once entered my *head* that I had promised to date him Friday, and when he came to the door about seven o'clock I was just *flabbergasted!* And here Bob was coming over at eight. I was just *desperate!*"

"So what did you do?" Peggy asked, wondering again why it was that some girls had the problem of too many dates while others the problem of none at all.

Alice didn't answer at first, and then her voice came hesitantly and shyly. "I stood there looking at him, with my mind scurrying around trying to figure a way out, without letting on I'd forgotten. After all, I didn't want to hurt his feelings and I thought, you know, if he got mad he'd never ask me out again. So I had just figured out something good and then —" Her voice faltered and stopped and then picked up again on an even softer note, "— and then I remembered I was a Christian and I just *couldn't* lie. So I told him right out that I was an idiot and always doing dumb things, and this was one of them, and I had this other date, but I'd *really* like to do something with him for a while anyway."

"Was he mad?"

"Well, you know how he gets. He was sort of stiff and formal, like people you read about in books, you know. And he said, 'Well, of course, if you would prefer not to spend the evening with me.' I could have died trying to keep from laughing, Peggy. Imagine saying, would you *prefer* not to! Most guys I know say, 'Do you want to or don't you?' But he is nice, Peg, in his way. So then, I just rattled on about nothing much — it's a good thing I'm good at that because he hardly said two words the whole time — and we went and had a soda, and I promised I'd go to the first basketball game with him."

"Oh, oh! You'd better not forget," Peggy warned.

"That's why I'm telling you now so you'll help me remember. And I've got it written on a piece of paper and tacked up on the bulletin board in my room. And I told Bob about it later so he wouldn't ask me."

"It must be rough to have so many dates." It was an effort for Peggy to keep her voice light and teasing, and it didn't help any for Alice to answer, "You're lucky you don't have the problem."

And then almost immediately she exclaimed, "Oh, I didn't mean that the way it sounded, Peg. You know I didn't! I just meant you wouldn't be so dumb and get into the messes I do."

"Just try me," Peggy replied, trying again for the light touch but not altogether sure she had kept the longing in her heart from showing in her voice.

"What are you doing tonight?" Alice asked quickly.

"Sitting with Linda and Barbie. The Andersons are going out for dinner. Ellen is coming over to keep me company. Anyway her mother is away, too. I would have asked you, but I thought you'd probably be sewed up with one of your many problems."

"I am, but this time it's with relatives."

"Your usual problem."

"You know it!" Alice exclaimed feelingly. "Actually though, they're not really a problem anymore. I mean, they *are,* but I try not to think of them like that. I just keep thinking how nice they would be if they were only saved. I mean, they're nice now, but they could be nicer, you know?"

"I know what you mean." Peggy thought of her father as she agreed. Then, catching a glimpse of her mother looking in from the kitchen, she added, "I've got to hang up, Alice, and get some studying done. I know with Ellen along tonight we'll just sit and talk after the kids are in bed. See you tomorrow?"

"I *think* so. My mother hasn't actually *said* yet that I can't go, and that's a pretty good sign. Some of my relatives are staying overnight and everyone sort of sleeps late then, so I can at least come to Sunday school. Even though all my aunts and cousins are around, my mother will probably want me to come home and help with dinner."

A shade of bitterness had crept into her voice, and Peggy felt sorry for her, as she did whenever she thought of Alice's mother. Mrs. Matthews was more bitterly opposed than ever to the church and everyone connected with it.

"Can you come to young people's?"

"I hope so. That's one reason I'm staying in tonight. Maybe, if I'm real chummy with the family tonight, my mother won't mind my going out tomorrow."

"I guess she doesn't like Bob any better yet?"

"No! She still blames him for what happened last summer and of course she thinks his religion is just a lot of baloney — not that she put it that way exactly." Alice sighed, and her voice was forlorn as she added, "There's nobody harder to convince with the truth than my mother. The funny thing is she used to swallow without a question all the stuff I used to tell to get out of a mess. But now when I tell the truth, she just gets suspicious."

Peggy glanced around again as her mother appeared in the kitchen doorway for the fourth time, looking very much annoyed. "I've really got to hang up. My mother wants the phone. See you."

"I don't want it," her mother answered the last remark. "But Bill is expecting a call. He saw an advertisement in the morning paper for a trumpet and called about it, and they're supposed to call back this afternoon. Though why he wants to fool around with it is more than I know. To say nothing of ruining our ears listening to him."

"He said he played at Uncle Ed's —"

"That battered up old thing wouldn't play very well," Mrs. Andrews interrupted scornfully. "All the boys in the family used it at some time or other, and it never played well to begin with from what your father has said."

"I guess that's why Bill wants a new one," Peggy argued.

"I should think he would have better use for his money — or rather, *your* money," her mother replied. "He said he was borrowing some from you."

"I should have been smart enough to charge him interest and make some money," Peggy said, trying to laugh her mother into a better mood.

But instead Mrs. Andrews complained, "It wouldn't be quite so bad it he were going to do something useful with it. But he only wants to play for church meetings."

"Well after all, you wouldn't expect him to join a — a jazz band or something," Peggy protested.

"I still think he could find something more practical than wasting time and money for a trumpet for church meetings."

The finality in her mother's voice left no invitation for argument, and Peggy started silently upstairs. It was probably only Bill's personality that had kept her mother from a flat refusal in the first place.

She stopped at the top of the stairs as the phone rang, and she heard her mother answer, "No, he isn't here. Very well, I'll tell him."

She looked up at Peggy. "You'd better draw out your money. That was the boy who has the trumpet. Bill can have it for eighty dollars if he wants it. I hope he looks at it carefully and doesn't just snap it up. It's probably in no better shape than the one at the farm."

"He'll certainly try it out first," Peggy answered. "My goodness, Mother, he's not a child any longer. He's old enough to make some decisions for himself."

"Sometimes I wonder," her mother retorted grimly, and headed back to the kitchen. Peggy watched her go and sighed again. Poor mother! Always a pessimist.

3

A Teacher's Scorn

Peggy walked slowly toward school one morning the next week, feeling the tangy nip of the cool air even through her crimson wool sweater. It was the kind of crisp golden day that would have teased one into believing that cold weather would never come, if it were not for the masses of leaves that drifted against bushes and caught around the tree trunks, leaving the bare arms of the trees as mute warning of the coming winter storms.

She turned to look over her shoulder several times. She had waited on the corner as usual as long as she dared and still leave time to get to school without rushing. This was the one place where Alice hadn't been successful in changing her habits since she was saved, Peggy thought now, with a faintly exasperated smile. She still could never quite make it to a place on time.

Catching sight of Ellen waiting in the middle of the next block, Peggy quickened her steps with one more glance backward.

"Where's Alice?"

Peggy threw her hand out in a gesture of disgust. "Recombing her hair or trying a new shade of lipstick or something, I suppose. She'll come tearing along pretty soon, never having any idea it was so late and so on. You know her."

Then she looked at the sheaf of notes clutched in Ellen's hand and the book that was propped open and balanced precariously on top of her notebook. "You're not still studying?"

"Yes! Peggy, I'm scared stiff!" she moaned. "I didn't know anything about government when I started this course, and I know even less now after all the haranguing old Verbeck has given us in the last seven weeks or so. I know I'll flunk this test. I know it!"

"No, you won't." Peggy tried to be reassuring. "Just don't get rattled. We went over all this stuff together yesterday, and you knew practically everything then. Just keep telling yourself there's nothing to be scared about."

"But it's what I don't know that he'll ask," Ellen answered gloomily. "It always works that way for me. Let's face it, Peg. I'm just not the intellectual type."

"If you think *you* aren't, what about me?" Alice asked from behind them and they both turned around in surprise.

"Where'd you come from?" Peggy asked. "I've been craning my neck around to look for you every couple of seconds, but you were never in sight."

"I got a late start and was hoping to catch up with you and was tearing along like crazy when Larry came by and picked me up. Then I had him drop me off when I saw you. I've been cramming every second."

"What was he doing around here?" Peggy couldn't help asking, as one part of her mind wondered longingly why something like that never happened to her.

"I don't know. Didn't ask. I was too busy going over this list of dates. Do you think he'll ask them all?"

"Probably — and others we've never heard of. Did you stay up late to study?" Ellen asked.

"Kind of," Alice answered. "And then I set my alarm

for five and went over my notes again while I ate a grapefruit and —"

"I don't get it," Ellen broke in. "I thought you said you got a late start."

"Oh." Alice looked embarrassed and then said haltingly, "Well, I did get up early to study and then just about the time I was leaving to meet Peg, I realized I'd forgotten my devotions because I'd been so busy thinking about the test. So — I was late," she finished.

They had pushed in through the stream of kids in the halls and as they did, Peggy kept thinking of the change that had taken place in Alice in the last few months. She was thinking about it so intently that she forgot to be careful as she opened the locker door and had to duck to avoid the book that slid from the top shelf and hurtled toward the floor.

Alice grabbed the book and promised guiltily under Peggy's accusing eye, "I *will* clean it out today, Peg. Or anyway, tomorrow at the latest."

The test was hard. Peggy knew she had passed it safely though she had chewed her pen over the one essay question that had been included. It wasn't that she didn't know what to say, but it was hard to express yourself on that kind of a question. But she felt sorry for Ellen, sitting next to her, who used her eraser as much as her pencil, and felt especially sorry for Alice, who looked sick when she finally got through.

But the test was nothing compared to the scorn of Mr. Verbeck when he returned the papers a couple of days later. He was indignant at the low grades as a reflection on his teaching ability. Then, as he lectured them on their poor study habits and their inattention in class, he really warmed to his subject and in blistering language excoriated them for their lack of knowledge of their government and of world affairs and, most of all, for their indifference to that lack.

"It's one thing to be ignorant," he stormed, "but it's another thing to know you are ignorant and not care to do something about it. Here you sit as the most favored group of young people in the world as far as your opportunities and privileges are concerned. And what do you do about those opportunities? Nothing! Nothing! Such a waste! Such intolerable lack of appreciation! You have the priceless gift of a free education and you're blind to it."

He looked around at them with unutterable scorn mirrored on his face, and the class members, though used to his lectures, looked at one another uncomfortably. Then his voice took on a quieter but more intense quality.

"What does your government assure you by its very constitution? Life? Liberty? The pursuit of happiness? Yes, all of these. And in those brief words lie all the hopes and dreams and visions — yes, the lifeblood of the people who gave everything they had for these dreams. And they didn't do it for themselves only but for all the generations to come — so that you could sit here and enjoy in peace and security what they fought and died for."

His voice was angry and accusing as he bit out his next question. "What is the most important of these three benefits to your generation? I'll tell you. It's the pursuit of happiness. *Your* happiness. Your own personal satisfaction is the only standard your generation has. And what happiness someone else enjoys is only important to the extent in which it affects yours. What do you care that millions of young people are old by the time they are teens — old because of squalor and misery and disease? Why should you care about the misery of your counterpart in a mud or grass hut across some continent? Do you ever think of the one whose home is the freezing outdoors and whose bed is the hard ground and whose dinner is cast-off garbage? Does it matter to you that there are hungry minds and hearts around the world? Or that the yearning of these minds to be filled is greater than the yearning for a full stomach? To these, just to barely maintain life is a consuming problem. And what is your most important problem?"

His eyes swept over the room as he paused momentarily, and his voice was scathing as he answered his own question in barbed words. "It's how to worm through this course with a low C. Or how you can work on the old man to get the car again tonight. Or —" his eyes rested on Alice in the front row — "or whether or not you'll get a date tonight."

His hand struck the desk sharply, and he asked passionately, "Do you know what freedom is? Can you appreciate freedom from want when you have never known what it is to be torn apart by hunger? Can you appreciate your freedom of speech if you have never had to live under the tyranny of a secret police?" His voice dropped to a lower pitch as he asked, "Can you appreciate freedom if you have never known the oppressive shadow of a constant, continual, corroding fear?"

The bell that rang then was a jarring note in the utter stillness of the room. But its shrill disturbance brought the class back from the spell of the unknown evils which hung threateningly close, to the welcome relief of known reality, and there was an urgent jostling to leave the room as quickly as possible.

But Peggy and Ellen, coming from their seats near the back of the room, reached the desk just as Alice, standing hesitantly beside it, said gravely in a low voice, "Getting a date really isn't the most important subject for most of us, Mr. Verbeck."

His smile was sarcastic and his voice purposely disbelieving as he asked, "Oh, isn't it?"

She shook her head. "I guess most of us aren't as serious about life as we should be. But it is hard to be serious about those things if you don't have to be, isn't it?"

It was obvious that he was impatient at having to continue the discussion with someone he considered immature, but Alice stubbornly stood her ground.

Peggy was amazed to hear her say earnestly, "There's something else I was thinking about while you were talking. There's one freedom you didn't mention. That's freedom from sin, and it's about the most important one there is. If you have that, the others don't really matter, do they?"

His smile was still sarcastic. "Obviously you have never been hungry or oppressed or fearful." His voice held a question and Alice, hesitating a moment, finally shook her head. "No, not really."

"Then you don't know what you are talking about," he answered. His voice was sharp and bitter as he added, "I have known all three. This is not mere theory with me." He gave an abrupt motion of dismissal, and the girls turned toward the door.

Then Alice half turned toward him again and asked, "But do you know anything about freedom from sin? In your own life, I mean?"

His head jerked up and he searched her lovely, expressive face for evidences of impertinence but saw only a troubled concern. He didn't answer but continued to stare at her. After an uncomfortable moment of silence,

Alice went on, "Because, you see, I do know this freedom so I *can* talk about it. And it *is* the most important." Then she added, "And it's only found in Jesus Christ."

Again there was no answer, and Peggy, listening to and watching the strange scene, was barely conscious of the people brushing past them to fill the room for the next class. It seemed to her that in that brief moment of eternity the simple faith of a new Christian had met the derision of unbelief and had been triumphant. For Mr. Verbeck, as cynical as ever, said, "I never would have guessed that a face as pretty as yours guarded such deep and serious thoughts." But the amused cynicism in his voice was offset by the expression on his face which held surprised respect.

This time his dismissal left no room for further discussion, and the girls hurried to get to their next class. "Boy! That's one way to get a teacher to notice you!" Ellen exclaimed. "How did you ever get up enough nerve to do it?"

"I don't know," Alice answered slowly. "It — it really wasn't nerve. I mean, if I had stopped to think about saying anything, I probably wouldn't have. It — well, it just seemed as though this was something maybe he didn't know about. I've always felt kind of sorry for him, haven't you?"

"No!" Ellen exploded. "I only feel sorry for the ones that have to have him for a subject."

"Don't you, Peg?" Alice appealed. "You can tell these things mean a lot to him. Didn't he come from Holland or someplace? That accent he has when he's mad is from someplace. He's probably had a lot of hard experiences and doesn't know about the Lord."

Peggy nodded, but didn't have time to answer as she

went into math and Ellen and Alice crossed the hall to
lit class. She was glad there wasn't time to say anything
because she couldn't have answered in a steady voice.
Her throat was tight from a conscious effort to keep
control of her emotions. All through the years that Alice
had been her closest friend she had unconsciously agreed
with her mother's often expressed, contemptuous dismissal
of Alice as a scatterbrain. No one had ever taken her
seriously or given her credit for being anything but a
very pretty girl with a beautiful voice and a love for a
butterfly existence.

And yet she had done something that none of the rest
of them had thought of doing. Alice, a Christian for not
quite three months, had spoken to someone about Christ
— simply because it needed doing — when she, a Christian
for over three years, hadn't even seen the need. Peggy
felt completely humbled.

Her mind reverted to the test papers Mr. Verbeck had
handed back so scornfully. Glancing at hers she had
found the A she had expected. But across the bottom
of the last page at the conclusion of the essay question,
he had written in his bold strokes, "As usual this is well
thought out and well expressed. But you wrote with your
mind and left your heart out completely. This was supposed to be a discussion of *people,* not of stick figures!"

She had felt resentful. But now, bending over the geom-
etry problems and reexamining her answer in the light of
the disturbing pictures he had raised in class, she had to
admit, in all honesty, that he was right. She had written
out a clear and logical answer to the problem he had
raised. Yet actually she acted as though the plight of
the other half of the world were only a question for her
to deal with on a test paper; she had been comfortable

in the knowledge that it wasn't necessary really to come to grips with any of the problems. And she was ashamed that Mr. Verbeck should be so concerned when she and other Christians she knew were not.

She remembered, too, his utter fury one day in class when the same subject had been under discussion and one of the fellows had shrugged off the problem of the starvation diet on which so many existed with the flippant comment, "So what? What can we do to keep the world from starving? Send them our leftover meatballs?"

The class, while smarting under the verbal blistering Mr. Verbeck had proceeded to give, had been stirred to heated discussion with an awakened sense of responsibility. But Peggy realized now that her own interest had been only intellectual and academic. She hadn't really cared.

And yet she found herself asking, "But what can I do? What can one person do that would make any difference?"

She raised the question the next Sunday morning in class, sure there must be an answer to the problem somewhere in the Bible but not sure how to go about finding it.

Miss Method thought soberly for a few minutes before answering slowly, "I wish I could give you some easy, pat answer. But I can't, because there isn't an easy answer. In a way, this is a problem that every one has to figure out the answer to for himself. Some do it by —"

"Yes, but if God wants us to do something for people doesn't He tell us what?" someone interrupted impatiently.

"And how?" someone else added.

The teacher shook her head positively. "If you expect to find in the Bible a blueprint for an answer to every wrong or injustice or problem in life, you'll never find it. It just isn't there. The Bible doesn't give a detailed plan for curing all the social and economic wrongs in the world." She looked around at them seriously. "Remember, though, that the Bible gives something far more important, and that is the remedy for sin. And sin is the cause of all the other wrongs in the world."

"But people don't automatically become rich or have enough food and clothes when they become Christians," Ellen objected.

"What you are saying is that if sin is the cause of wrong, then not being a sinner should make everything right." Miss Method's look was quizzical and Ellen said, a little doubtfully, "Well, yes, I guess that's what I mean."

"It does make you right with God. But, you see, there will always be wrongs and injustices in the world as long as sin is here. And sin is here until the Lord Jesus returns again. Only then will sin be gone and, with it, hunger and thirst and fear."

The words brought back a reminder of Mr. Verbeck, and Peggy said impatiently, "But *this* is what bothers me. Do we just wait until then? I mean, do we just let people go on being hungry and not do anything about it?"

"Absolutely not!" Miss Method was emphatic. "In fact, the Bible warns us that if we do that, we are not living as a Christian should."

This was what Peggy wanted. "Where does it say that?" she asked eagerly.

"In James 2:15-17." Miss Method read the verses aloud slowly, " 'If a brother or sister be naked, and destitute of daily food, And one of you say unto them, Depart in peace, be ye warmed and filled; notwithstanding ye give them not those things which are needful to the body; what doth it profit? Even so faith, if it hath not works, is dead, being alone.' "

"But I don't know anyone who is hungry or anything,"

Ellen protested. "It's not our fault if there aren't any around us." Then she said, "Well, I suppose there are, but not like the people Mr. Verbeck was talking about. Really *starving,* I mean."

"People do send money to other countries though, don't they?" Alice asked. "And packages of food?"

Miss Method nodded agreement as she said, "That's what I was going to say when we first started on this. Some people find an answer by helping to support a child and send money to pay for his clothes or food or education. A little of our money goes a long way in some of these other countries."

"Could we do something like that?" Peggy asked. "Our class, I mean?"

In the enthusiastic response that came with the suggestion, Miss Method looked around at them thoughtfully. "You understand that if you start this you would have to do it every month. You couldn't send money one month and not the next, or half of the amount sometimes instead of all of it."

They all agreed, and Ellen said, "I'd want it to go for some kid's food instead of his education. I mean, if a person was starving he wouldn't be crazy over getting just a book."

"All right," Miss Method agreed. "But there is one string I would like to put on this as a — oh, maybe as a test for each of you. When we have settled on how much money we will give each month, we can figure out how much each of you must bring to meet it. But I would like your money to be a sacrifice for you."

There was silence for a moment and then Ellen asked "You mean, not ask our mother for something extra?"

"That's right. Nor take it out of baby-sitting money or allowance or anything like that."

"How are we going to get it then?"

"By going without something," she answered quietly.

"You mean like food?" Ellen's voice squeaked.

"You might be supporting a child who has one meal a day at the most. Would it hurt you to do without a meal once a month?"

In the startled silence that followed and as the girls looked uncomfortably at each other, she asked, "Do you think you could bring yourself not to buy the new sweater you think you need so desperately so that a child can have a pair of shoes instead of walking through the snow with rags tied around his feet? It's easy to do something for someone if you don't have to give up anything yourself because of it. But I would like you to really go without something to help someone else. Each one of you can decide for yourself how you want to work it out."

"We'll be showing him — or her, whichever it is — how to be a Christian too, though, won't we?" It was Alice asking and Miss Method nodded.

"From what you have said about your class, Mr. Verbeck feels that physical hunger is the most important need. There is something far worse, and that is spiritual hunger. Along with the food we provide for this child, we must also show him how to be saved."

"When can we start?" Ellen asked with her usual practicality and directness.

"I'll get a letter off today to several organizations that work overseas and see what children are available. What age would you like if we have a choice?"

"Why not some cute little kid about three or so? The pictures you see in magazines are so sweet when they look out at you with such big, solemn eyes," one of the girls said.

"I think it should be a girl about kindergarten age or so," was another suggestion.

"Would there be a girl about our age?" Peggy asked thoughtfully. "Some one like that, we could each write to her, and we would know — I mean, we would have the same kind of reactions to things. It would be more personal that way."

"She'd probably be glad to get letters from American kids," Ellen put in.

Miss Method looked at her oddly for a moment before answering. "Probably there are not many available who are that old," she frowned in reply. "By the time young people are in their teens in other countries they have taken on more responsibilities and are more self-sufficient than you are. But I'll ask," she promised.

As Peggy bowed her head in prayer with the other girls she wondered fleetingly what Mr. Verbeck would say if he could know of their plan. He had once spoken very scathingly of people who "salved their conscience" by sending a food package at Christmas to someone in need, and she couldn't help wondering if that were what they were doing now. But then, of course, they would be sending her a Bible or tracts or something too along with the money. That should make a difference.

4

The Treasure Hunt

Bᴵᴸᴸ ᴡᴀs ᴏɴ ᴛʜᴇ committee that was planning the postponed treasure hunt, and they had set it for Friday evening. He was so mysterious about the details that Peggy refused to give him the satisfaction of knowing she was dying of curiosity. Wednesday, as she went past his room, she noticed a white envelope lying on a chair near the door with the word, CLUES, printed on it. She gave a quick look around to make sure he wasn't there and then opened it.

A single sheet of paper was inside, and after she had unfolded it, she stuck it back in the envelope in disgust when the words, "Ha! Ha! I fooled you, snoopy!" stared up at her.

It didn't help any to have Bill come bounding up the stairs, just as she came out of the room, trying to look innocent. "How juvenile can you get?" she asked in response to his triumphant expression, and the look she gave him should have dropped him on the spot.

But the committee had done a good job both in their planning and in the publicity they gave it. A big bunch of kids turned out so that the six cars they had rounded up were really loaded. Peggy couldn't imagine by what wild streak of luck she had gotten assigned to Larry's car next to Ann, with two other girls and Dan in the back seat.

When everyone had piled into the cars, Bob stuck his

head in the open car window next to Larry and asked, "Got enough room? We'll take one more person if you're crowded."

"No, we're okay," Larry answered, but Bob persisted, "No sense in bunching up if you don't have to. How about it?"

Peggy leaned forward to look at Bob and, from the corner of her eye, she could see Dan in the back seat sitting very aloof from the rest. She felt sorry for him and wished Bob would go on. There just wasn't any sense in making Dan miserable. He was probably dying to be in the same car with Alice and was too proud to let on. Not that it would help him any with Bob around. With Bob gone on her, who else would stand a chance?

"And anyway," she thought, "Alice and Dan just aren't the same type. He might as well give up his dreams about her."

"Well, anyone coming?" Bob asked again, and Ann teased, "How can you need anyone else when Alice is with you?"

"Oh, we've got other kids along." He fooled around with his car keys, not looking at her as he answered, "I just didn't want to overload this car when we have room for one more."

One of the girls in the back seat leaned forward to peer out the window at his car parked beside Larry's and exclaimed, "You're crazy! You've already got seven in there — eight with you. We only have six."

"Oh." Bob turned red. "Oh, yeah, I guess you're right. I didn't count straight, I guess. Okay. Let's go then."

"We have to wait for the signal to start," Larry said. "Who's giving it?" he asked peering through the windshield.

"Bill," Peggy answered. "And if he doesn't do it pretty soon, he'll burst! He's been keeping secrets on this thing for two weeks."

"That brother of yours is really going places, Peggy," Larry said as Bob went back to his car and they got the go-ahead sign. "He's getting that trumpet to really do things for him. He says he puts in the time practicing though."

"Don't I know it!" Peggy retorted feelingly. "We don't need alarm clocks at our house anymore with Bill blasting out first thing in the morning. I used to sort of like to wake up and listen to the birds chirping. But not any more! We can't even hear them now. Bill starts right in as soon as he's up, and we can't get away from it. He's even got my father shaving in rhythm with him."

"It's paying off though," Larry said again. "He's really making progress."

"Oh, sure," Peggy agreed. "But naturally I wouldn't admit it to him."

"I thought he sounded real neat in young people's last Sunday," one of the girls in the back seat said admiringly.

Peggy half turned to see which one it was, for she didn't know either of them very well. It was, she thought, the one they called Candy. As Peggy caught a glimpse of her vivid pixie face, she remembered Bill's words about not wasting his time on goofy girls and choked back an impulse to laugh out loud. Maybe he wouldn't have very much to say about it.

She sobered though, thinking that it didn't do *her* any good to like someone. She simply couldn't bring herself to be as frankly admiring as this little freshman was. It was too serious a matter with her. Maybe she ought to make more of an effort to get Larry to notice her, but she simply couldn't. Like getting into the car just now, she thought. She remembered how Alice used to maneuver it so that she would be the one to sit next to the boy she was currently interested in and did it so that only the girls noticed it — and were burned up about it. But Peggy couldn't make herself use those tricks.

Larry braked the car suddenly, jolting Peggy out of her thoughts, as Ann exclaimed, "Wait! Here, I think this is it," and she read out the first clue.

And this began a chase that took them from the greenhouse at one end of town, down to the bus depot, out to a large stone wall behind the public library, over to the band shell in the park, and finally to the attic in the church. Dan, surprisingly enough, and the little pixie were the best at figuring out the clues.

When they finally raced down into the church basement, sure that they were the first ones in, they were disappointed to find another team in ahead of them, already enjoying the prize, a huge pizza, which had been divided among the seven members of the group.

"You know, Bill," Peggy said, "you were pretty sharp. Those clues were tricky." Then she looked over her shoulder at Candy and added, "Next time you work on something like this, there's a gal who can give you some help. She really used her head tonight. She's the one who figured out most of the stuff for us."

"She did, huh?" said Bill as he grinned at Candy. She dimpled back at him, and Peggy watched with amusement as Bill casually strolled over toward her.

"What are you, a matchmaker or something?" Ann asked from behind her. Peggy laughed.

"No, but my insufferably smug brother thinks he's immune to all the girls. I just wanted to prove that he was wrong. Not that he'll ever admit it, of course. When he does ask some girl to marry him, he'll probably insist he's just doing it to be friendly."

"You've got an awfully nice brother," Ann remarked. Peggy wanted to say just as casually, "So have you," but didn't.

The committee in charge of the food had been generous in their estimates, but every one was starved and the miniature hamburgers some of the mothers had fixed disappeared in a hurry. Some of the fellows bragged they had eaten twelve, and one claimed fourteen.

"Naturally, it *would* be Bill," Peggy snorted.

When they had eaten and stacked what dirty dishes there were in the kitchen to be cleaned up later on, they moved over to one end of the room which had been fixed up as a sort of lounge. The girls flopped down in the wicker furniture with most of the fellows settling themselves on the floor. Ann automatically headed for the piano and played some choruses until everyone had gotten a place to sit.

"We've got a surprise act for tonight," said Bob, who was acting as m.c. "Let's give them a hand," and he led the applause for Bill, Jim, Dan, and Tom, who came out with such crazy stunts that they left everyone weak with laughter just because they were so silly. They ended up with a couple of numbers on their instruments and even Peggy, listening with a sister's critical ear, had to admit that they sounded good together. Each one seemed sensitive to the others' mood and blended well, with an unexpected sense of harmony.

"I think they've done a pretty good job of relaxing everyone even if they haven't exactly put us in the mood for something serious," Bob said as the four fellows got out of the silly outfits they had thrown together on the spur of the moment, and came back to settle on the floor with the rest of the group. "Maybe we could sing something. How about starting with 'He Cannot Fail'? Then you come up with your suggestions."

One song and chorus followed another until Bob, stopping to wait for another choice, was interrupted by Candy. Her pointed little face under its cap of smooth black hair was serious in spite of the dancing light in her eyes.

"I've just got to say something," she burst out. "You don't know how much it means to me to get into a church like this. It's *exactly* like ours back home. We just moved here last month, and I cried buckets. I didn't think I'd ever find a church as good as mine, and I didn't see how I'd ever find anybody in school who was a Christian."

She stopped and looked around mischievously. "Do you want to know how I did? Well —" She stopped and shot Bill a quick look.

Peggy looked over at him and had to bury her face against her arm for an instant to keep back a laugh at the sight of his rapt expression.

"Well," Candy was going on demurely, "I had to go to school early one morning and I was going by this house and I heard someone playing, 'Abide With Me.' And I knew right away that it had to be a Christian doing it. I mean, after all, 'Abide With Me' at seven-fifteen in the morning! And it was a rainy day too. So the next morning I went by the house again only this time about fifteen minutes later to see if it might be someone who was going to school. Well, I did that for about a week and a half —"

She stopped and smiled at the laughter that rippled around the group and then went on, "And then one morning this girl came out, and it was Peggy, but she wasn't carrying an instrument and anyway, I knew it *had* to be a boy playing — I mean, you can sort of tell, can't you?"

The laughter was louder this time, and she appealed, "Well, can't you?" And then she went on, "So I kept walking by, and then one morning Bill came out, and he was carrying his trumpet. So I found out who he was and started coming here because I was sure it would be a good church if someone like that came here. And it is," she finished triumphantly.

"If Bill is embarrassed at being the object of such attentions, he certainly doesn't show it," Peggy thought, amused.

One thing Candy had done was to break the ice, and there was a companionable sharing of thoughts and testimonies. Peggy couldn't remember that they'd had a time quite like that before. She was glad now that the committee hadn't planned a special program, since everyone seemed so relaxed and willing to share with everyone else.

It was Larry who brought the serious note into the evening when he said, "You know, I was thinking about what Candy just said, that she didn't expect to find a church like the one she came from. I suppose we all feel that way pretty much. Getting in with a new bunch isn't always easy. I know when I think of leaving here next fall for college — well, it looks kind of grim, you know? I guess we'll all have to do what Candy did —"

"You mean, find a girl who goes to a good church and follow her?" Bob interrupted, grinning.

"That's what I had in mind, although maybe not *quite* that specific," Larry said before getting serious again. "It is important that we get in with the right group, not just here at home, but especially when we're away. Those of us going to a university might find it pretty rugged if we had to go it alone."

"And that's the best part of it, isn't it?" Ann asked softly. "I mean, that we don't have to go it alone. Even if we do leave our church and home and friends behind, the Lord goes right along with us. If we let Him."

"Like that fellow — What's his name?" Bob asked. "The one who slept on a stone? I've got it — Jacob. I still get some of those names mixed up," he muttered, embarrassed. "Anyway, he found out that he couldn't get away from God no matter where he went."

"I'm glad God wouldn't let me get away," Alice's voice was serious. "When I think of how much happier I am right now than I ever was before —" Her shoulders rose and fell in a gesture that said more than words could. She appealed to Ellen. "You know that poem we read in lit the other day? It says just exactly what I mean. The poet said he was running from God because he was afraid if he gave in to Him he wouldn't have anything. Uh — let's see if I can quote it —"

"Lest, having Him, I must have naught beside," Ellen broke in in a gruff voice.

Peggy, looking at her and remembering how unsentimental she was, knew the poem must have made a terrific impression on her. Ellen and poetry ordinarily just didn't go together.

"That's it," Alice exclaimed. "I thought you lost out on all the fun when you were a Christian. I thought all you could do was just sit around and talk — like this. And yet, actually, that's all we did before, just sat around and did goofy things in the drugstore and got everyone mad at us."

When the party broke up a little later Ann said, "Peggy,

would you mind giving a hand in the kitchen? The kids who were going to do it have to get right home. Larry said he'd help since he doesn't have to take anybody home. It shouldn't take very long."

Peggy was thinking that with Larry there she wouldn't mind how long it would take, but only said, "I'll tell Bill to go ahead."

When she got out to the kitchen, Larry was running water into the dishpan and dumping in soap flakes. He looked around at her. "Are you one of the wipers?"

"Or, I'll do the washing."

"I told Ann I would. Keep you girls from dishpan hands —" He stopped as Bob looked through the serving window and asked, "What gives out here?"

"Clean-up crew," Larry answered.

"Who's on it?" Bob asked and looked around as Ann came through the door and grabbed a dishcloth. "Need any more help?" he offered.

"We'll be through and out of here before you get Alice to her front door," Larry jeered.

But they had hardly made a dent in the silverware before the outside door opened and Bob came tearing in, pulling off his jacket. "Okay, tell me what to do."

"What got you back here so fast?" Larry demanded.

"Alice had her usual deadline, so I figured there was no point in hanging around, wasting my time," Bob explained offhandedly. "Here, I'll sweep up."

He grabbed a broom, but, instead of sweeping, he lounged in the doorway, watching and talking as Larry washed and the girls wiped and put away dishes and cleaned up the counters. Peggy mostly listened while the others talked about college.

Larry had long ago put in an application at the state

university. Peggy had heard him tell someone that since he was going to seminary afterward, he wanted to rub shoulders in college with kids who didn't know anything about Christ so he could know firsthand how they thought about things. Ann had applied at a Christian college downstate and was hoping to hear any day that she had been accepted. Then she asked Bob where he had applied.

"I — uh — I put in an application at a couple of places," he replied as he turned the broom handle around and studied it intently. "I figured I'd better because I might have trouble getting in. You know, I don't have such a hot record." He wasn't bragging, simply stating a fact that had to be admitted. "It isn't that my grades are so bad, at least not so far this year, though they're not like Peggy's here." He stopped and grinned at her and she asked, "What do you know about my grades?"

"Your little friend brags on you all the time. She's got you slated for valedictorian next year."

"How about that?" Larry asked admiringly, and Peggy felt her cheeks get hot. But she couldn't help wishing that he were admiring her for some other reason than her brains!

The dishes were finished and Larry was dividing up a stray bottle of coke he'd found in the refrigerator while Bob was explaining to Ann that it was the stuff the teachers had written about him in his file the last couple of years that might give him trouble in getting into college anyplace.

Then Larry leaned an elbow on the counter and asked, "Where else have you applied? I knew about the university and that place down south. Anyplace else?"

But Bob, instead of answering, put down his glass

abruptly and said, "Look, I'd better finish this up so we can get going," and he began sweeping vigorously.

Larry stood watching him with, Peggy thought, an odd expression on his face. Larry seemed engrossed in his own thoughts as they came out of the church and stood waiting while he locked the door. Then, walking to the car, he seemed to make a sudden decision and said, "Look, how about sharing your car, Bob? Why don't you take Ann home? I'll take Peggy. You girls don't mind being divided up like this?" He looked from one to the other and Peggy was glad she didn't have to answer as Ann said with a laugh, "Trust my brother to make my decisions for me," and walked with Bob to his car.

Peggy got in the car as Larry held the door for her, wondering what this was all about and wondering if her dreams were coming true after all. Larry drove in silence for several blocks and then smiled at her as he said, "I think there must be some kind of magic about your family."

"Magic?" Peggy's voice was a squeak as she repeated the word.

"Yes." He looked over at her. "Did you see Bill's face when Candy was talking?"

She nodded. "I wish I'd had a camera. He'll never believe he was so hypnotized, and by a girl at that."

"I couldn't help laughing at her frankness in telling how she followed him to his church. And then I looked around at the bunch and was thinking how much it has grown in the last few years and how many new kids we have. Most of them came in after you did. So you really started it all."

"Bill was first, though, really," Peggy said.

"And then Ellen and Alice and Bob. And Dan, I forgot about him. And those two girls Ellen brought."

"Plus the girls who come because Bob does, don't forget them," Peggy laughed. Then she added seriously, "But it was what we found here that did it. This church and your father's preaching have been — well, they've really been terrific. I hate to think that in one more year I'll be going away to college, too, and leaving it all. Although it won't seem the same next year with you away — all of you, I mean," she added hastily.

They had stopped now in front of her house and Larry reached to turn off the ignition as he said, "It's funny how things work out. I'm thinking of the way people change and the — the unexpected way events happen that you can't foresee."

He still seemed bothered by something, and she couldn't figure out what it was until he asked abruptly, "What's Alice planning on doing? When she graduates, I mean?"

"I don't know. She doesn't either, exactly."

He drummed his fingers on the steering wheel and stared off into the darkness, and Peggy felt a flare of resentment. She wondered why it was that all the guys talked to her about other girls as though she were a stick with no feelings of her own! But out of loyalty to Alice she swallowed hard and went on in as normal a voice as she could, "Her whole outlook has changed so much since she was saved, that she hasn't had a chance to think about the future. Before, she didn't plan on college because she's not very crazy about school. She thought she'd get a job for a little while and then get married. But now —" She stopped and shrugged.

"She dates quite a bit, doesn't she?"

"Yes, not so much now. I mean, not so many different

fellows. Mostly now she goes with Bob and sometimes with Dan."

"Is she — I mean, does she — like Bob pretty well?"

Peggy managed to squeeze out the words, "I think so," past the tight feeling in her throat as she thought she saw the drift of the conversation. Larry was interested in Alice too! "It isn't fair!" one part of her mind kept saying. Why should Alice, who didn't really care, have all the fellows falling for her? She would never make a good minister's wife, never!

Through the haze that seemed to surround her, she was aware that Larry had gone on talking and was saying, "A Christian ought to pray about it and be sure of the Lord's will. After all, we pray about other things and this is one of the most important, don't you think?"

She nodded and after a moment said, "I suppose sometimes we don't pray about it because we're afraid He won't answer the way we want Him to."

"I suppose so." He was still wrestling with his problem and said, "The thing is, sometimes you date someone and they like you better than you like them. Then they end up getting hurt if you find out you like someone else. That's why I like my system better than Bob's. I figure it's better to wait until the right girl comes along and you're sure about it and then take her out."

"You're sure you'll know the right one?" she asked wistfully, with an ache in her heart.

He nodded positively as he got out to come around to open the door and take her up to the porch. "Thanks for letting me sound off, Peggy. You're an easy person to talk to."

Peggy closed the front door behind her and leaned

against it for a moment "I don't want to be an easy person to talk to!" she whispered. "I want to be liked, for *myself,* not just because I'm somebody's friend!"

She was glad the rest of the family were in bed and the house was dark except for the tiny stairway night-light her mother left on whenever someone was out. After a moment, she dragged herself wearily upstairs to bed and, finally, to a troubled sleep.

5

Breakfast-Table Conversation

Peggy got up quickly and padded across the room in her bare feet to turn off the alarm and close the window and then looked longingly at her warm bed. It took everything she had to resist the urge to crawl back in and pull the covers up and refuse to face the world. It was one of those days. She looked out the window at the steel-gray sky, which was letting through light but no sunshine, and shivered. The trees looked forlorn with their bare branches exposed to the cold wind and the soggy leaves huddled around the base against the bare hedges. It certainly wasn't the kind of a day that would send a person's spirits soaring.

Then she resolutely went to the bathroom for a quick, splashing shower, remembering how foolish she had been in other years to let the weather affect her outlook. She could remember times when she had moped around all day just because it looked a little bleak outside. That had been true even after she had been saved. She felt a little foolish, remembering, and was glad she was over that stage at least.

Something in the back of her mind reminded her that it was just about as silly to let the fact that she was still dateless affect her moods too, but she pushed the thought away. After all, that was something that could affect one's whole life. It was important, too, no matter how much Mr. Verbeck might sneer at it, nor how much Larry might think all you had to do was wait for the right person to show up.

The thought of Mr. Verbeck brought the reminder that by the end of the week she would have to have her contribution for Myling Han. The almost-sixteen-year-old Korean girl whom the Christian agency had found for them, was tiny and fragile. Her enormous eyes, looking out at them with a hauntingly frightened expression, had the girls exclaiming over how pretty she was even though her appearance was so foreign. They had sent one check, and Alice and Ellen had gotten together and written her a letter telling about themselves. But they received back a carefully worded letter in English that was very distant, cool, almost ungracious.

"She certainly doesn't sound very grateful!" Ellen exclaimed, and Miss Method, looking around at the circle of indignant faces, had asked quietly, "Is that what you wanted from her? Gratitude?"

"Well, yes," Ellen insisted. "It wasn't any fun giving up — what I did," she finished hastily. They had agreed they wouldn't tell how they were raising the money.

"What did you write her?"

"We really didn't know what to say," Alice replied. "We finally sort of introduced ourselves and told about some of the things we do —"

"And tried to sound as though we really wanted to be friends with her, you know," Ellen broke in.

"Perhaps whoever writes next should try to imagine you've lived for sixteen years like she has and see if it makes any difference in your letter," Miss Method suggested.

And now Peggy, brushing her hair carefully to keep from disturbing the new hair style that meant sleeping on one arm with her head up off the pillow, wondered ruefully if the venture was going to be worth all the effort that was involved in it. Whatever she sacrificed, she knew she would have to keep it quiet, for her mother would think the idea a lot of nonsense.

With a final look at herself in the mirror and the wistful hope that someday she might be satisfied with what she saw looking back at her, she went downstairs, sniffing the fragrance of bacon and fresh cinnamon rolls.

"They smell wonderful, Mom!" she said, reaching for a hot roll.

"And taste even better," Bill added. "Is there enough for a fourth?"

"I made them to be eaten," his mother retorted.

"Just three more weeks," Peggy said to no one in particular. Bill looked up and asked, "Till what?"

"Vacation! How could you forget? Just imagine having two whole weeks to laze around and only do what you want to." She sighed in anticipation. "The only books I'm going to read will be for fun." Then she frowned thoughtfully. "Dad, will you give me some help on writing to different schools for catalogs? I've got to begin to decide where I'm going."

"Already?" Bill asked.

"Already nothing! Some kids decided a long time ago. You can't wait until the last minute to apply and then expect to get in."

"Well, I suppose that depends on where you want to go," their father said, coming into the conversation with one eye still on the newspaper. "A topnotch place would be more selective than a second-rate school and would be harder to get into."

"The trouble is the topnotch places cost the most, I suppose," Peggy said worriedly.

"You can probably work part of your way," her father reassured her. "Lots of kids do. Or you might get a scholarship. I should think you would stand a pretty good chance of that."

"With my luck I probably won't," Peggy said morosely, sinking momentarily into her natural pessimism.

"Hey, what's with you?" Bill asked in surprise. "You're really a sad sack today."

"That's enough, Bill," Mr. Andrews warned. Then he added, "I suppose *you* have already made up your mind where you are going and have all the details worked out."

"Sure," Bill answered from behind a mouthful of sugared oatmeal. "First I'm going to Bible school —"

"*Bible* school! Whatever for?" his mother interrupted sharply.

Peggy looked fearfully at Bill, still engrossed in his food and seemingly unaware of the tone of his mother's voice, and then at her father, who was carefully stirring his coffee and not looking at anyone.

"Well, I figure if I'm going to be a missionary, I'd better get the right kind of training. You know, like a doctor goes to medical school and an engineer goes —"

But Mrs. Andrews, with a white, angry face, stood up abruptly and began to clear the table.

Bill looked up at her in surprise and opened his mouth to say something, but Peggy kicked him under the table and frowned at him as she swiftly shook her head.

"What's the matter?" he asked after his mother had gone out to the kitchen with a load of dishes, and without saying a word.

"Just keep still, won't you?" she muttered crossly, and then stood up with a quick look at the clock.

"We'd better step on it."

"If you don't, you'll be late for your meeting," their father agreed and added, "I'll drop you off on the way since I have to go early too."

"How does it happen you both have a meeting on the same day?" Mrs. Andrews asked from the kitchen doorway.

Peggy felt powerless to stop either the explanation or its results as Bill went up the steps two at a time, calling back, "It's our Bible study group that meets every Monday morning before school."

For a long moment Mrs. Andrews stood motionless and then said in a tight, strained voice, "I don't know how much longer I can stand this," and turned quickly again to the kitchen.

Peggy looked at her father, who shook his head helplessly and, after a moment of hesitation, got up and went out to the kitchen also. She couldn't hear what was said but knew from the expression on his face as he came back through the dining room and went to the closet for his coat that he hadn't accomplished anything.

"Should I go out and say anything?" Peggy asked, tying a scarf carefully over her hair.

He shook his head sadly. "I don't know if it would do any good or not," he answered, and then Bill clattered downstairs, zipping up his jacket and reaching for his gloves.

"Where's Mom?"

"In the kitchen," Peggy answered. Then she added quickly, "Come on. Don't make things any worse than they are!"

But he only sent her a puzzled look as he went toward the kitchen calling, "Mom, I'm staying for basketball. Anything you want me to do?"

Peggy turned abruptly and pulled open the door. "Think I'll wait outside," she said over her shoulder to her father, her voice muffled against her scarf.

"I'll go along too and get out the car. Are we stopping for Alice?"

"She said she was going." Peggy watched as her father opened the garage door and disappeared from sight.

The door banged behind her, but she didn't look around as Bill shrugged himself deeper into his jacket.

"Boy! Cold today," he offered.

"It's hot enough inside, thanks to you!" Peggy snapped.

"Now what did I do?" he demanded.

"You wouldn't understand if I told you," she answered scornfully.

"Girls are about the hardest people to understand there are!" he said feelingly. "Come on, Peg, give. What have I done?"

"You just don't have any — any tact or common sense or anything!" she stormed at him as she yanked open the front door of the car and got in. "Why do you *always* have to say something to get Mother upset?"

"You're crazy! She wasn't upset. Was she, Dad?" he appealed.

"Well, she could have been happier," his father answered wryly.

"She sure seemed all right to me," Bill insisted. Then, after a moment, "Anyway, I don't see what I'm being blamed for. What did I say that you think was wrong?"

"Talking about going to Bible school for one thing," Peggy answered heatedly.

"Well, what's wrong with that?" he demanded indignantly. "You were talking about going to college. You brought up the subject in the first place."

"Yes, but college and Bible school are two different things."

"I still don't see why one can be talked about and the other can't —" Bill began, but Peggy interrupted him fiercely. "They're different as far as Mother is concerned, and if you weren't so dumb you could see it."

"Wait a minute, both of you," Mr. Andrews broke in. "I don't think either one of you is willing to see the other person's viewpoint."

"As far as I'm concerned, he doesn't have any," Peggy muttered. "He's only making it harder to ever get a chance to interest her in Christian things if he has to get her all worked up over the subject just by being so — so bullheaded."

"That will do, Peggy!" her father said sternly. Then he went on, "You're both right, and you're both wrong. Bill is right to be able to talk about the subject so naturally. I'm just sorry I can't do it as easily as you can, Bill. But, on the other hand, Peggy is right in wanting to witness tactfully. It won't make your mother want to be a Christian if you just blurt out the first thing that comes into your mind without thinking of how it might sound to her."

He had been driving slowly and stopped the car now to turn and look at them seriously.

"I supose it's almost impossible for you to see your mother as anyone but just your mother. You would have to know her background to really understand why she thinks the way she does and acts the way she does."

Peggy and Bill could only sit and look at him wordlessly

as he stared off into space, lost to them completely for a few moments. Then, still as though he were a million miles away, he said softly, "She once had so much, and lost it all — and she has never gotten it back."

Then, with an effort, he shook himself loose from his memories, started the car, and drove rapidly to Alice's house.

"There she comes," Peggy said in a tight voice, glad the conversation could be stopped, even though the memories couldn't be. The sadness in her father's voice had roused an ache in her that combined with the almost intolerable feeling of guilt she was carrying these months. The hardest thing for her to do lately was to let others know that she was a Christian. She thought back to earlier years and couldn't remember any time when it had been so hard. It was strange, too, because this year all the kids she went around with were Christians and did things together.

Yet her lack faced her at every turn. Even Alice had the courage to speak to a teacher. And at home, Bill made it seem the most natural thing in the world to speak of Christ.

And here she was even finding it hard to give a testimony in the youth group and it wasn't because she loved the Lord less. It wasn't because she didn't want to. It seemed as though the timidity that had plagued her ever since she could remember even wanting to express herself, had closed in on her this fall and she couldn't shake it off. If she could only be free from this burden of longing that grew heavier every day! It seemed to be interfering with every part of her life. She wished again, as she had so many times in the past years, that God would make it as easy to *live* for Him as it was to be saved.

6

News from Aunt Emily

For some unaccountable reason, Peggy decided to go right home after school that afternoon. Alice had to detour around to her aunt's house to do an errand for her mother and asked Peggy to go along. Ordinarily she would have been glad to go, for this was the aunt who always seemed to have just freshly baked something rich and gooey whenever they stopped in. But this time she refused and was glad she had, for Bob dropped by the locker as they put on their coats and walked with Alice.

Ellen's mother had arranged to pick her up at the side entrance of school to do some Christmas shopping, and Peggy declined a ride with them in favor of walking home. She almost welcomed the feel of the cold air against her face and the sting of it on her hands. In the rush to get out of the house in the morning, she hadn't checked to see if her gloves were in her pocket. They weren't, and by the time she got home, her fingers were numb with cold.

She knew the minute she stepped inside the front door and saw the letter propped on the telephone table, that her mother would not be in a very happy mood. It was from Aunt Emily. The decisive, angular writing that was so characteristic of Aunt Emily always gave Peggy a chill feeling of foreboding, whether it was deserved or not.

The letter was addressed to her mother only, as usual, a fact which never failed to irritate Peggy. It always seemed to symbolize the utter disregard of her aunt for her father, as though by not acknowledging him, she somehow made him not exist.

Peggy frowned now as she looked at the envelope, for Aunt Emily's letters were not usually left out in the open like this. Fortunately she did not write often, and Peggy was glad of this, for the letters when they came always made her mother unhappy and brooding.

As she hung up her coat and scarf in the closet, she heard her mother come downstairs, and turned toward her with a smile.

But the smile faded and her sense of foreboding grew stronger, for the usual straight line of her mother's mouth was even more rigid as she indicated the letter with an abrupt, angry gesture.

"You might as well read it right away. There's no point in hiding bad news."

"Has something happened to them?"

"Read it," Mrs. Andrews answered shortly.

Peggy picked up the envelope and took out the letter, unfolding the single heavy sheet of stationery. The faint fragrance of perfume her aunt always used drifted up and brought memories of Aunt Emily's personality.

The letter was brief and to the point.

DEAR ELIZABETH,

Unless your plans preclude your having us as company, Walter feels that we owe you a visit, though why, after all these years, I do not know. We have discussed the matter thoroughly, but he is quite adamant about having his own way in it in spite of my wishes. He and Jane both want to come, so I have little choice.

We shall, of course, stay at a hotel so that we shall not inconvenience you in any way. Jane may

prefer to visit with Peggy, but there is no need for
us all to crowd together for the time we are there.

I shall let you know the exact time of our arrival,
which I trust, will be only a day or two before
Christmas. I shall see to it that the whole visit will
last not more than a week.

I am sure this will be no more welcome to you
than it is to me, but we will both have to make
the best of a bad situation. I have never known
Walter to be so insistent before. Why, I say again,
I do not know.

Peggy took longer than was necessary to read the
letter, not knowing what kind of reaction was expected
from her. Now she looked up.

"It will be — nice to see them," she finally ventured
hesitantly.

Mrs. Andrews took the letter and reread it, and then,
as she thrust it back into the envelope with an unsteady
hand, she said, "I'm going to write and tell her not to
bother coming."

"Why?"

"Why?" her mother cried in echo. "Because she doesn't
want to! She couldn't have made it any plainer. And,
anyway, you've been out there. You know how they live!
Think what a contrast it is to this!" and her hand swept
over the living room contemptuously.

Peggy looked around the room. They had had the
chairs and sofa as long as she could remember, but they
were comfortable. And they always looked nice with the
two sets of slip covers her mother had made, a solid dark
green for winter and a light floral pattern for summer
wear. It was true that the piano was old and hard to
keep in tune and had a few keys that stuck occasionally,
but it always had a high glossy sheen that matched that

of the coffee table and the two end tables. Peggy knew her mother disliked the drapes because they were home-made, though so skillfully done anyone might have thought they had been hung by an interior decorator. The whole house was a shining reflection of Mrs. Andrews' passion to do everything perfectly.

Peggy frowned as she looked around, not wanting to argue about it and not wanting to make her mother more upset.

"You see?" her mother said, following the movement of Peggy's eyes.

"Well, I was thinking — I mean, I think it looks very nice," she answered defensively.

Her mother made a futile gesture of despair with her hands and Peggy added hastily, "Of course it doesn't look like Aunt Emily's house does. But not very many places do. I mean, most of the people we know have houses like ours instead of like hers. And anyway, Uncle Walter can afford to give her that kind of house and everything that goes with it and Dad can't. Aunt Emily knows that."

As soon as the words were out of her mouth, she wished desperately that she could take them back. That was about the worst thing she could have said to her mother, for it brought up unpleasant memories and opened old wounds that Peggy knew existed but didn't completely understand.

"Exactly!" Mrs. Andrews retorted in grim agreement. "That's exactly what she knows. But I'm still not eager for her to come and see it for herself."

"Hasn't she ever — I mean, they've been at our house *sometime,* haven't they?" Peggy asked diffidently.

"Not since Jane was a baby," her mother answered

shortly and turned away so abruptly that Peggy knew better than to ask any more questions.

"Well then, why don't you just write and tell her it won't be convenient for them to come —" Peggy began, but was interrupted by the impatient shake of her mother's head.

"I can't do that, much as I would like to. When Emily has made up her mind to something, it's impossible to change it. I should know that. I grew up with her," she said with a bitter note in her voice. "I'll just have to work it out the best way I can and try not to mind her looks and comments."

"I'll help clean the house," Peggy offered.

"Cleaning won't cover up the ragged and worn places." Her mother was fretful and discouraged-sounding as she looked around again. "But I guess that's the only thing we can do. At least they won't be staying here the whole time, thank goodness!"

"Will it be all right if Jane does though?"

"Yes, if she really wants to," was her mother's somewhat reluctant answer.

Peggy was surprised at her own eagerness for the anticipated visit. She was sure it would work out better than the last one had, four year ago. For, even though the house and their circumstances were the same, they had changed. She and her father and Bill were new people because of Christ, and even Jane could be expected to be more responsive since her contacts with Lisa and Uncle Walter and Mrs. Tremont and Sally.

Peggy picked up the letter again and read through it thoughtfully and felt her pulse quicken at the prospect of the visit. She wondered, would this be the way God was working out her mother's salvation? It seemed impossible for that ever to happen, and yet the impossible happened all the time. It had with Uncle Walter, with Ellen, with Alice, with Dad —

"There is every reason to hope that it will happen with Mother and Jane," she thought and felt a thrill of anticipation begin to rise in her. "And maybe this is just the way God has it planned."

But the anticipation was almost lost in the hectic activity of the next few weeks. Peggy had experienced her mother's frenzied cleaning sprees before. But nothing in the past was like what they were doing now, she thought in despair, as Christmas grew closer and her mother bent every effort to make the house gleam. She began at the top with the attic, rearranging everything in it and washing the windows and curtains. Then she moved next to the upstairs, moving all the furniture out of each room and even out of the closets and scrubbing and waxing and painting everything in sight. She somehow found time to make new curtains for the bedrooms, maintaining scornfully that the old ones were only rags anyway.

Every day when Peggy came home from school she found her mother either cleaning out kitchen cupboards or washing walls and windows or studying the living room furniture with a frown, trying to decide how to rearrange it to show it off to its best advantage. She had excused Bill from helping until school was out, since he had basketball practice every afternoon, on his promise that he would really pitch in and help the last few days before they came.

Peggy had promised to help Mrs. Anderson with the primary Sunday school department during vacation and especially help with a party she was giving for them several days before Christmas. Now, as Peggy went to sit with Linda and Barbie, she explained her problem to Mrs.

Anderson, who listened sympathetically and nodded understandingly.

"If they come that day, don't worry about it. I'll find someone else to take your place for the party. What about Ellen?"

"Put her in charge of the games, and she'll do a good job even though she pretends she can't stand kids," Peggy laughed, remembering their experiences in the nursery school last summer. Then she sobered and said, "I do want to help my mother all I can." Quickly she added, "Though sometimes I think all of us just get in her way," thinking of her mother's impatience the evening before when Bill, insisting on trying to help her move something out of one cupboard to another, had dropped a treasured teapot. In catching that almost miraculously, his elbow had brushed against some cups, and they had shattered on the floor.

Peggy had stood by in helpless sympathy as Mrs. Andrews exclaimed, "*Please,* let me do this myself! Then I'll know it's done right." And she had added with the accustomed touch of bitterness in her voice, "I wouldn't mind it so much if all the effort were of some help. But all the polish and wax in the world won't hide the fact that we have nothing!"

And Peggy had remembered again the sad words of her father, "She had everything and lost it all." She had never prayed more earnestly in her life than she had last night that the emptiness and futility in her mother's life might be replaced by the joy and satisfaction of knowing the Lord Jesus.

As she hurried home from the Andersons, she again prayed fervently for her mother. Each day they were expecting further word from Aunt Emily, with Mrs. Andrews dreading its arrival.

Peggy went in the front door so she could see at a glance if there were any mail, for it irritated her mother these days every time someone asked if there were any news. No letter was in sight, and Peggy was glad for another day's delay.

Her mother called from the basement, "Turn on the oven, if that's you, Peggy. And put in the casserole if I'm not up in about ten minutes."

When she came up a little later she brought two small boxes and, in answer to Peggy's questioning look, she said, "I remembered today that I had put these away somewhere. They are full of recipes that I haven't tried for a long time. I haven't been cooking anything fancy in recent years, so there was no reason to have the boxes in the way." She flipped through some of the cards with an abstracted, "I wonder, where *is* that one for Christmas dessert?"

As they finished dinner, Mrs. Andrews looked over the recipe file again. "If I just knew how many meals they will eat here," she fretted, "it would make it easier to plan. They will be here for dinner Christmas day, of course, but I don't know how many other meals to insist on."

"Why not just wait until they get here and sort of ask them at the last minute?" Bill suggested.

Both Peggy and her mother looked at him pityingly, but neither of them answered. Mr. Andrews, with a wry smile, said, "That's one department that you and I had better keep out of, Bill."

"Yes, your job is to get the basement in shape and that will keep you busy enough." When Bill opened his mouth to protest, his mother went on, "No arguments, please, Bill. I was down this afternoon and realized what a mess it's in. You'd better start in Saturday if you expect to get it done before they come."

"Before they come?" he repeated. "Aunt Emily won't go down *there,* will she?"

For some reason, Peggy's glance strayed to her father's face. The look she saw there made her struggle with inner amusement. She was sure he was no doubt contrasting, as she was, Aunt Emily's fastidiousness with the appearance of their basement.

It was such a contrast that she smiled involuntarily and her father, seeing her, broke into a sudden shout of laughter and laughed until he was helpless, with Peggy joining him, first with a giggle, and then in a laugh that left her with tears running down her cheeks.

But they sobered instantly as Mrs. Andrews got up from the table and said coldly, "When you two are through with your private joke, you may do the dishes, Peggy. I am going upstairs to plan the menus if you think you can do without my company."

"I'm sorry, Mother," Peggy said contritely. "It really wasn't funny. It was just the idea — I mean, Aunt Emily and the basement —"

"Never mind the explanations and excuses," her mother replied, still in the same measured tone as though she were fighting to hold on to her self-control. "I feel the same way myself when I think of Emily coming into this house. Except that instead of laughing, I could cry!"

Peggy and Bill and their father sat in sober silence as Mrs. Andrews picked up the recipes, went upstairs, and closed the bedroom door behind her.

7

Alice Tells Peggy a Secret

THE IMPENDING VISIT became, to Peggy, a monstrous shadow hanging over them and blotting out all thought of anything except housecleaning. She would hardly have known it was Christmas if it weren't for the decorations on the streets and in the stores, and the mad rush of shoppers. She had gotten a gift for Lisa and mailed it Saturday morning with postoffice warnings in her ears that it was only thirteen days until Christmas and packages that went any distance might not arrive on time unless they were mailed immediately. But as far as her mother was concerned, Christmas preparations were important only as they related to the coming company.

Peggy and Alice went downtown to shop Wednesday afternoon, the first day of vacation, and on the way Peggy confided to her some of the problems they had been having. "At least having my relatives here gives me a little more time to think of what to get them," she finished.

"That never helps me any," Alice answered. "I never can come up with anything new or different."

"Of course, you have so many," Peggy sympathized. "All I know about are my aunt and uncle in California and then Uncle Ed and his wife, where Bill was the last couple of years. There are some others, but we've never kept in touch with them."

"You're lucky you don't have the pack that I do!" Alice exclaimed.

"You don't give presents to all of them, do you?"

"We used to, and that was murder! My mother used to make my sister and me start in right after Thanksgiving to make presents. You know, pot-holders for my aunts and — oh, I don't know — little pieces of junk that my uncles pretended to be crazy about on Christmas day and then stuck away, and after a while my aunts would throw it out just in time to do it all over again the next year. Now each family buys things for one other family, and that works out better. I usually end up giving the same thing each year. I figure it doesn't matter since a different person gets it each time."

They walked along in companionable silence, each one busy with her own problems, until Alice said hesitantly, "I'm scared about my present this year though. I know Aunt Janet will blow her top, and my uncle won't even know what it is at first."

"Why? What did you get?"

Alice gulped as she answered. "A Bible. You see, none of them has one," she went on with a rush of words, "and I thought they should have at least one in the house, and I knew they would never buy it for themselves, and after I had thought and thought about what to get, I hit on that idea. Not that they'll think it's much of a present. And, of course, my mother is going to be furious! She thought I had wasted my money when she found out I had bought myself one at the end of the summer."

Then Alice went on in a burst of confidence that made Peggy feel more sorry for her than ever and thankful that at least her mother wasn't like Mrs. Matthews. "You know, at first I thought I would hide it — my Bible, I mean — and in that way avoid a lot of talk. But then I thought it would be worse if my mother found it. She'd know I was hiding it from her, and then I really would be in trouble. And anyway," she finished practically, "I couldn't think of any place to put it that she wouldn't look."

"Does she still do that? I mean, does she think it's right to look in your stuff even now when you're older?"

"Oh, sure. She thinks it's part of her duty to keep track of us. She doesn't know that we'd be glad to tell her things if she just trusted us a little. This way you feel as if you *had* to hide things. You know?"

Peggy nodded soberly and then suddenly Alice's irrepressible laugh brought the question, "What's so funny?"

"I was just thinking of what Bob told me about what his folks said the first time they saw him reading a Bible. They thought he'd really flipped because nobody ever would have thought he would want to read the Bible, the way he used to be. I guess it took them a long time to get used to the idea. They're still not, really, but at least they don't get mad at him for doing it." Her voice was sad as she finished, and it was obvious she was thinking of her mother's reactions.

Trying to change the subject, Peggy asked, "Wasn't that his sister in church a couple of Sundays ago?"

"Yes. He finally talked her into coming. I think she liked it all right, or at least she said she did, and she's coming to the next party." Alice giggled again. "Bob is such a scream! He has the funniest way of putting things and keeps you laughing all the time."

"I've been going to ask you if you still have his ring?"

"No, I gave it back to him pretty soon after I was saved. It was — oh, I don't know — sort of a symbol that I was different." She was embarrassed as she tried to explain. "Giving it back was, I mean. When I had it before, I'd hidden it from my mother and only wore it when Bob and I were out together. So I gave it back. He didn't want to take it at first, but then he decided maybe it would be a good idea. We're not really going around very much together anymore anyway," she added, almost as an afterthought.

"Oh, no! Just every place you go!" Peggy retorted.

"No, really. We just happen to have study hall and lunch the same periods. And then sometimes he takes me home or asks me to a game or something. But we're just good friends."

"Pretty *good* good friends, if you ask me."

"No," Alice insisted. "It's just that he knows me better than most of the other girls because we dated before last summer." She sighed then and said rather wistfully, "I wouldn't mind going steady with him, but—"

Peggy waited and then asked, "But what?"

"Oh, I don't know," Alice answered vaguely. "I think he's interested in someone else." Then, almost as though it weren't important, she added, "He and Larry are good friends, you know. I guess Bob goes over to the Parkers a lot — for different reasons."

The significance of the last part of the sentence was lost on Peggy as her mind drifted dreamily and her heart did crazy somersaults again at the mention of Larry's name. She thought guiltily of Mr. Verbeck's accusation, aimed at Alice, that the most important thing she thought about was getting a date. If he only knew! It wasn't Alice who did that; it was she.

She wondered ruefully how many hours a week she had wasted in futile daydreams that some day Larry would ask her for a date. The only consolation she had had so far was that he didn't date anyone really and didn't seem interested in anyone. He had been impartial to all the girls and nice to everyone, from the brains to the dopes and from the glamour girls like Alice to the ugly ducklings like herself. But now, remembering what he had said in the car, she was sure he had made up his mind. But the question was whether he could beat out Bob. Even if she didn't have his ring, Alice was still the one he dated.

Then Peggy came back to the present with a jolt when she realized what Alice had just said. "Bob? Ask Ann?" she repeated stupidly.

"That's what I've been talking about so mysteriously for the last five minutes," Alice answered and added quickly, "But don't spread it around. I don't think he's ever had a date with her really."

"You mean he wants to go *steady* with her?" Peggy asked, still feeling as though she must be hearing things.

"Well, he hasn't exactly *said* so," Alice replied cautiously. "But I finally began to catch on that he liked her because he talked about her so much. You know how guys are."

Alice stopped, and Peggy nodded although she didn't know, really.

"Only I don't think he knows that I caught on," Alice went on.

"How long has this been? That you think he liked her, I mean?"

"Oh, I don't know. Since school started, I guess. He'd just sort of mention that he'd been over at Larry's and what a swell guy he was. And then pretty soon — in the same evening, this was — he'd say what swell doughnuts Ann could make. And there I sat, not even able to boil an egg — or at least so my mother says. Finally it got to the place where he spent more time talking about Ann when

he was out with me than anything else. And I don't think
he even knew he was doing it. That's one reason I gave
back his ring. After all, there's no point in keeping a guy's
ring if he's going to sit around and think about some
other girl!"

They had reached Alice's house, and Peggy looked at
her friend in the growing darkness. She thought of the
many times through the years they had stood outside
each other's house for last-minute confidences, and smiled
a little as she realized how these confidences had progressed from simply moaning over a lost tennis ball to a
hashing over of parental rules and now to more serious
thoughts of the future.

"Do you mind?" she asked, feeling a little as though
she were prying, and yet remembering how freely Alice
shared secret feelings with her. "You and Bob have been
going around together for quite a while."

Alice kicked at the frozen ground for a moment and
didn't answer. Her head was partly turned away and Peggy
couldn't see her face. Usually Alice showed all her emotions on her expressive face. Finally when she did look
around, her face only looked thoughtful.

"No, not really," she finally said slowly. "At first I was
kind of mad about Bob's always talking about someone
else. Usually the fellows paid attention to me when they
were with me. But then — Oh, I don't know, Peg. It's
hard to explain, but you see things differently when you
are a Christian. Even things like dating, I mean. You feel
more generous about things. Know what I mean?"

Peggy shook her head. "No, I don't." And she hoped
Alice would explain.

"Well, I don't know about other girls, but before I was
saved, I wanted to have all the fellows like *me*. And the

girls I was running around with last year and the first part of last summer were like that too. I mean, everybody was sort of clawing to be at the top of the heap. You always were looking out for yourself. You never felt you could let down and just be yourself and be nice to anyone. You had to pretend all the time."

She stopped and looked at Peggy earnestly. "Could you imagine being jealous of Ann?"

Peggy shook her head.

"You see, there's a difference in your viewpoint when you're a Christian. You want other people to have the best, too, as well as yourself. And if Bob likes Ann better than me, well —" She stopped, and then said, "You'd never believe how much he has changed, Peg. He and Ann are really a lot alike now."

They parted after a few minutes, and Peggy hurried home, but again she felt as though she had sat at Alice's feet and had been taught something unexpected and, in its way, very wonderful. Alice was a constant surprise these days in her understanding of people. Peggy had never expected Alice could be like this.

But the news made Peggy look at Ann in an altogether different light. She had always thought of her as just Ann, nice and sweet and, in her way, sort of pretty so that you forgot about the slight limp that showed up, particularly when she was over-tired. Her friendliness had attracted both Peggy and Alice to church to begin with, and they had found it hard to resist her warm smile and generous personality. Her gift of being able to play any piece of music on sight had always kept her in demand at parties and meetings, but aside from that she wasn't particularly talented in any way. Again Peggy wondered, enviously and longingly, what it was that made some girls attractive to the fellows while some girls weren't even noticed.

And it was surprising that Bob, of all people, had fallen for Ann! Peggy watched Ann as she sat at the piano the next Sunday morning, noticing how absorbed she was in the music. Again Peggy thought how strangely things sometimes worked out. She turned her head slightly to look past Ellen, sitting next to her, so she could see Bob sitting in the back row on the other side of the room with a bunch of his friends. She deliberately kept herself from looking on down past two other fellows to where Larry sat.

And again came the overwhelming wonder that God could do anything. For who ever would have thought, knowing Bob a year ago, that he would become a Christian and be almost the most active senior in the whole youth group, and now be liking quiet, serious Ann. Again Peggy looked soberly at Ann. She had long envied Alice's easy and unplanned conquest of practically every boy around, knowing that Alice couldn't help that she was born pretty and had a sparkling personality that drew boys like bees to honey. All the girls were used to that. But here was Ann, without lifting a finger, attracting one of the most popular boys in the whole school. As she went to her class, Peggy gave herself a mental shake and forced herself to pay attention even though it took concentrated effort.

But she couldn't help noticing the rest of the day how many times Bob seemed to be looking at Ann and how much he hung around where she was, even when she was with a bunch of girls. As Peggy thought back now, knowing what she did, she realized how much that had been true in recent weeks. The way he had acted the night of the treasure hunt, for instance, made sense now. But along with that thought came the sickening realization that with Bob liking Ann, Alice was free for someone else to like. Larry would have a clear field. Bitter resentment flamed in her at the thought. Maybe Alice could be generous toward Ann and not be jealous of her. "But I can't! I can't!" she told herself miserably.

Peggy watched Ann at young people's that evening, trying to detect in her an awareness of Bob's interest. Apparently Ann had not been blind to him either for, as he stopped her outside of church after the service was over and said something to her, she nodded at him with a smile. Then they turned from the group gathered on the church steps and walked slowly along the quiet street, each apparently oblivious of the powdery snow that gently sprinkled them with a white coating. Peggy felt the familiar ache grip her throat and the nameless longing well up inside her. She wondered despondently, was she destined always to stand on the fringe of this mysteriously intriguing world?

The conversation of the other kids swirled around her unheeded as she looked from the two figures walking into the dusk to Alice, standing just across from her. Alice had tilted her head back to laugh at what someone was saying. The flakes of snow that hung on the tips of her long eyelashes were like starry points.

Peggy looked abruptly away. "Want a ride home, Ellen?"

"Sure. Are you going now?"

"My dad looks as though he's ready," Peggy answered as her father came down the steps.

They walked around to the parking lot with Ellen chattering away about the retreat and worrying aloud, "I sure hope you can go, Peggy."

Peggy, her mind still filled with visions of a bleak future, answered absently, "I do too." Then she shook herself free of her dark thoughts and said, "But it all depends on how long my aunt and uncle stay. My mother says we absolutely can't go if they are still here. I can see that I can't go off and leave Jane when she'll be here such a short time."

"Maybe she'll want to go too," Ellen said.

"Maybe," was all Peggy could answer. She wished the solution were that easy.

"I don't expect them to stay long," Mr. Andrews said, opening the car doors for them. "Your aunt said they would be here just a few days before and after Christmas."

"When do they come?" Ellen asked.

"Wednesday, I guess."

"Well, that should clear it then. Friday is Christmas, and if they stay until Sunday or Monday and we don't go until Wednesday, then you're safe."

"I'm hoping anyway." Then she said to her father, "If you're waiting for Bill, don't. He's with some of the guys and said he'd be home by nine-thirty."

They pulled out of the parking lot and turned up past the front of the church and Mr. Andrews slowed down as he looked out the window, peering through the flakes of snow that were piling up against it. Then he pulled on faster with a faint grin on his face. "I thought I'd offer Alice a lift," he said back over his shoulder, "but it doesn't look as though she needs one."

Peggy hadn't turned her head to look, but Ellen had and laughed easily as she answered, "That's one gal who'll never have to look for offers of a way home. They practically come and fall in her lap."

Peggy wished she could care as little as Ellen seemed to. But she *did* care and couldn't pretend not to.

8

A Special Delivery Letter

THE SPECIAL delivery letter that came Monday evening from Aunt Emily changed everything drastically.

Bill tore downstairs to the insistent ringing of the doorbell about ten o'clock and came back to the foot of the stairs to call up, "Mom! Special delivery for you. From Aunt Emily. At least, I suppose it's from her — anyway, it's from California."

Mrs. Andrews hurried downstairs with Peggy crowding after her and Mr. Andrews coming up from the basement.

They watched as Mrs. Andrews tore the envelope open, read the short letter quickly and silently and then sighed with relief. "This is certainly an answer to prayer," she said with a short laugh and handed the letter over to Mr. Andrews. He, too, read it silently, and then passed it to Peggy to read, with Bill looking over her shoulder.

"I'm sorry," Mr. Andrews said. His wife retorted, "Well, I won't pretend that I am!" Then she added, "Oh, I'm sorry Walter is sick, of course, but I'm glad it has kept them from this visit. You will never know how I have been dreading their coming!"

But Peggy by this time had taken in the other news in the letter and broke in exclaiming, 'But Lisa's coming! Did you see that? In their place! With Jane, I mean. Isn't that wonderful?"

"I don't see that it is at all wonderful — or necessary,"

her mother answered stiffly. 'The last time Jane came, she came alone. And she was younger then."

"I guess Aunt Emily is doing it for Lisa's sake," Peggy began, but her mother shook her head firmly.

"There must be some reason for it," she said, and little lines of worry creased her forehead. "Emily never does anything without a reason."

"Well, I'm not going to stew around about *why* it's happening," Peggy bubbled happily. "I'm just so glad she's coming. How'll we work out the sleeping arrangements, Mom?"

"That's exactly what I'm wondering. We simply don't have enough room for two extra people."

"How about —" Peggy began, but Mrs. Andrews was going on deliberately, "Jane will share your room, of course, just as we had planned originally."

"I thought —" Peggy bit her lip, and stopped when she saw the expression on her mother's face.

"And there isn't room enough in it to put up a second bed, even temporarily," Mrs. Andrews said, and Peggy realized she had known that was what her mother was going to say. For some reason she was not welcoming this visit from Lisa, and even sounded angry about it, evidently just because Aunt Emily had suggested it. Peggy decided there was nothing she could do about that.

"She can have my room," Bill offered. "I can bunk some place else for a few days."

"Absolutely not!" his mother answered sharply. "We're not going to have you move out of your own house for a perfect stranger!"

"Well, I could use my sleeping bag at night in the hall or someplace," he offered.

"No!" was the explosive reply, and Bill subsided meekly as he caught the warning look his father gave him.

"We don't have to decide sleeping quarters right now," Mr. Andrews put in. "Let's think about it overnight at least. When will they arrive?" He looked at Peggy, who still had the letter clutched in her hand.

"Let's see — Thursday. Thursday noon at 12:25. But they get to stay all next week.

"This means a complete change in plans," Mrs. Andrews was fretting. "It's too bad we couldn't have known about it before now. We could have saved ourselves a lot of work."

"Yes, it's too bad Walter wasn't considerate enough to get sick sooner," her husband commented dryly.

"That's not particularly funny," his wife retorted. "And that isn't what I meant. But just remember that you weren't the one who slaved to get the house in shape for company."

"A lot of what you did wasn't necessary," he observed.

"It was necessary for Emily," she replied stiffly.

After a moment her husband nodded. "Perhaps you're right. It was necessary — for her."

"I still say what's-her-name can have my room," Bill put in. "She has to sleep somewhere."

"Bill, will you please leave that to me?" his mother demanded. "Since she is coming and we can't change that, we'll have to do something with her. But please give me a chance to work it out."

"Okay. But don't say I didn't offer," and he clumped upstairs to the milk and sandwich he'd been devouring when the doorbell rang.

Peggy followed him upstairs, her eyes bright with this unexpected and wonderful development. It took her a long time to go to sleep as she tried to figure out a way to get her mother to change her mind about Lisa.

When she finally opened reluctant eyes the next morning, she tried to shut out the sound of the noise downstairs, and turned over to drift off to sleep again until the memory of the letter made her sit bolt upright, her arms hugging her knees as she thought, "Lisa is actually coming in two days!" Then she looked at the clock. "Almost nine-thirty. Think I'll call Ann. She'll flip too when she hears about it."

She pulled on a robe and felt under the bed for her slippers, and padded downstairs, stopping in the middle of a yawn to exclaim, "So this is what all the racket is about! I couldn't imagine what was going on down here."

Her father only grunted from where he was stretched out full-length on the floor, tightening the screws on the Christmas-tree holder. "How's that?" he asked. "Is it straight now?"

"Yeah, I guess so," Bill answered, looking at it critically. "Sure, it's okay now."

"That's not a bad-looking tree," Peggy observed. "It's sort of small, but otherwise it's all right."

"What do you mean, 'small'?" her father asked indignantly. "As it was, I had to cut off some of the top to keep it from scraping the ceiling. We don't want a lot of marks on this new paint job!"

"No, I guess not. Anyway, a tree always looks different with lights and ornaments. And we do have a thing to go on the top, don't we?"

His eyes twinkled up at her as he asked, "Didn't you make an angel or something when you were in fourth grade?"

Peggy's, "Don't be silly!" and her mother's, "Don't be ridiculous!" came at the same time. Then Mrs. Andrews said, "I bought some new ornaments last week and threw out some of those old ones you insist on putting on year after year."

"You shouldn't have thrown them away," her husband protested. "Some of them had a lot of sentiment attached to them."

"They were pretty tattered-looking," she retorted. "I certainly wasn't going to have Emily see those old things."

Peggy sat on the arm of the sofa, swinging her leg back and forth, not taking part in the conversation. She was remembering the Christmas tree at Aunt Emily's the year she had lived there and how it had seemed like a decoration piece rather than a reminder of what Christmas was about. She could almost feel now the lump of longing she had then for the old, homemade, funny decorations her father liked so much. "I certainly take after him in that way" she thought, and felt a little ashamed that she was glad she did.

Then, remembering the reason for coming down, she said, "I'll help fix the tree as soon as I make a phone call."

As she dialed Ann's number, she again felt rising excitement at the prospect of Lisa's coming, and the eagerness spilled over into her voice as Ann answered.

"Guess what?" she said abruptly. "I know you'll never believe this but it's true. Lisa is coming for a visit. On Thursday! Yes, really, it's true."

She stopped at the exclamations coming from the other end of the line, completely satisfied with the response the news had brought.

Then, in answer to Ann's question, she said, "No, my aunt and uncle aren't coming after all. My uncle is sick and is in the hospital. My aunt didn't say exactly what was the matter. Anyway, that's why Lisa is coming. Jane wants to and she is keeping her company on the trip. Lisa is keeping Jane company, I mean. I'm so excited I can't talk straight!"

From behind her, she heard her mother say, "I still think it was a completely unnecessary precaution. What will we do with her?"

"I don't think you need to worry," her husband answered. "Apparently the girls are crazy to have her. They'll make some kind of arrangement probably."

"I should think she would want to spend the holidays with her own family instead of going off with complete strangers," Mrs. Andrews went on critically.

"Just a minute, Ann," Peggy said, and then turned to face them, covering the receiver with her hand. "We're not strangers! At least I'm not!" Then she asked, "You don't think there's *any* way we can possibly manage for her to sleep here?" Her voice and eyes pleaded for a yes, but her mother shook her head decisively.

"Not if you can make other arrangements. And, Bill, don't mention your sleeping bag to me again," she warned crossly, as he started to speak.

"Okay," Peggy sighed regretfully. "Ann begged to have her stay there. She's asking her mother now." She listened into the phone again and said, "Okay. I'm green with envy, but since we don't have room here I'm glad you're the one to have her. And, of course, she will be glad, too. Look, come on over after a while and we'll make plans. Can you? Just think! Only two days!"

She frowned a little at the next question Ann asked and replied guardedly, "Well, I don't know. It depends on — on different things. Probably if Lisa is staying with you, she could, but I don't know about — about the rest of us."

Peggy hoped Ann would understand that she hadn't wanted to talk too freely about the retreat with her mother listening. She'd have to lay some ground-work for it before Lisa and Jane came.

"I guess Lisa won't mind," she said with a worried look as she turned from the phone to perch on the arm of the sofa again. "I mean, mind staying there when she thought she would be staying here."

"Mind?" her mother echoed with a trace of scorn. "Why should she? She's getting a free trip across the country and practically a two weeks' vacation out of it, don't forget."

"Oh, Mother! I don't see why you are taking everything out on Lisa! You don't even know her. And it isn't her fault that she's coming."

"I don't have anything against her at all. But I do think it's strange that you should be more concerned about her and more excited about her than you are about your own sister's coming."

Peggy was silent. Afraid that her eagerness at seeing Lisa would show up too much, she had tried to conceal it a little. She wanted to burst out and tell her mother the difference between Jane and Lisa and how much easier it was to get to know Lisa, and how much more they had in common since they were both Christians and Jane was not. She wanted to remind her mother that it wasn't her fault Jane didn't seem like a sister. It wasn't her fault that Jane had lived with Aunt Emily all these years so that she and Peggy seemed like strangers when they were together. But she kept still. It wouldn't really be possible to explain it anyway and, if she tried, it would only get her mother upset and rake up a lot of trouble. All she could do was hope that her mother's apparent dislike of Lisa wouldn't be too obvious.

Mrs. Andrews didn't wait for an explanation anyway. She got up abruptly, saying, "I don't know about anyone else, but I have a lot to do between now and Thursday noon. Peggy, when you're dressed, I have some jobs that simply must be done this morning."

"Be right there," Peggy answered. Then, as her mother disappeared into the kitchen and the sound of running water covered up her voice, she turned troubled eyes toward her father.

"I wish Mother didn't feel that way. I'd hate for Lisa to be hurt or know she wasn't wanted."

"Don't worry about your mother's attitude, Peggy," he answered quietly. "You don't know her very well if you think for one moment she would let on how she feels before a stranger. Your mother was raised in the kind of atmosphere where politeness, if not kindness, was important and where you masked your own feelings to carry out the idea of graciousness. There may be faults in that kind of philosophy, but there are virtues, too, in these days when we tend to blurt out how we feel without regard for someone else's feelings. Once Lisa arrives, there won't be a hint of all this."

Peggy looked at her father in perplexity. There was a note of pride in his voice about this that she would never have expected. Ever since she had been old enough to discern what was beneath the surface of her parents' conversations and be aware of the undercurrents of tension that often eddied between them, she had realized how different their viewpoints were. Her mother's background of wealth had left a stamp of snobbery on her. And her marriage had created a gulf between her and her sister that was as unbridgeable now as it had been twenty years before. And now here was her father defending this system!

Peggy watched him curiously as he gathered up his tools after a final shake of the tree to be sure it was solid. Then, as he went down to the basement, she sighed. There was no use raking over those old problems when they weren't hers to settle anyway, especially when she had enough of her own. She started upstairs and stopped irresolutely on the bottom step.

"I might as well get it over with right now," she muttered grimly and went out to the kitchen, glad that Bill wasn't around. He seemed to have a knack of speaking up at the wrong time and saying the wrong thing. She poured herself a glass of orange juice and then said casually to her mother's back, "This means they'll be here over the retreat next week."

Her mother didn't answer and, after a moment Peggy barged on, "I suppose if Lisa is staying with Ann, she'll be going."

"Peggy," said her mother, turning around to face her. "I know you think I'm very unreasonable about this subject. But I think you might as well make up your mind right now that you won't be going this year. After all, Jane will be here as a guest, and you simply can't go off and leave her for two or three days. I'm sorry, but that's just the way it is."

"What if she wants to go?"

Her mother didn't answer at first. She continued to look at Peggy's face and then said, "She probably won't want to. But if you insist on hoping for a miracle and end up being disappointed, that's up to you. You are old enough to make that decision for yourself. It seems to me it would be much more sensible to simply decide you won't be going and save yourself some heartache eventually."

Peggy finished her juice and rinsed the glass carefully.

Inside she was boiling at the callousness of her mother's disregard for her feelings, with a concern for only Jane. Peggy went upstairs and let off steam by scowling at herself in the mirror and brushing her hair so hard it hurt, and she gradually calmed down. She realized with a feeling of shame that her mother had unwittingly given her the clue to the solution of the problem. Instead of just hoping for a miracle, she should pray for one.

"Why is it you automatically stew around about things instead of praying about them without being reminded?" she asked her reflection severely.

The answer came unbidden, and she pushed it away as she turned from the accusation in her own eyes. But it was there in spite of her efforts not to put it into words. She knew she was afraid to pray, for fear God wouldn't answer the way she wanted Him to. Just as she hadn't really prayed about this other burden that weighed so heavily. What if the answer should be no?

9

Lisa and Jane

M<small>RS.</small> A<small>NDREWS</small> had been sure that the weather, which so far had been unusually mild for December, would be bad, for there were reports of a storm coming in from the northwest. She anxiously peered out the window just before going to bed Wednesday night.

"It looks all right yet," she said with relief. "I hope they aren't grounded someplace or won't be terribly late getting in."

"If that should happen, I'll bet Jane will be glad Lisa is along for company," Peggy couldn't help remarking, and her mother gave a grudging nod of agreement.

But Thursday, though very cold because of a sudden drop in the temperature, was crisp and bright and when they reached the airport all flights were reported on schedule.

"I'm so glad it's sunny!" Peggy exclaimed as they stood by the gate after the flight had been announced. "Everything looks so much better when the sun is shining."

"I'll bet they'll think it's cold no matter how sunny it is," Bill observed. "And anyway, the sun won't look like so much to them when they have it all the time."

"That's my point," Peggy retorted. "Imagine coming from sunshine to what it *can* be like here in winter. That's why I'm glad it's sunny today."

"I wouldn't trade it though," Bill argued. "I like variety and —"

He was interrupted as his mother exclaimed, "There they are! Isn't that Jane? There, I mean, in the blue coat!"

Peggy stood on tiptoe to look, and Bill said in a troubled voice, "I don't remember her well enough to tell from here. But there are two of them together," he added helpfully.

"Yes!" Peggy said suddenly and positively. "That's Lisa with her. Let's go out. But don't holler at them, Bill. They'll see us in a minute."

"I'm like Bill. I'd like to holler," her father said grinning at her. "Why be afraid to show them you're glad to see them?"

"Of course, we want *them* to know that," Peggy answered. "But think what people would think if we all started yelling, 'Yoo-hoo,' or something like that!"

"And Jane wouldn't like it anyway," Mrs. Andrews agreed. "There's no need to make a spectacle of ourselves just to show them we're glad they are here."

They crowded out the door, feeling the bite of the cold air on their faces, but to Peggy, excited and keyed up as she was, the coldness felt good against the flush of her cheeks. She realized, as she looked out at the girls approaching them, that subconsciously she had been afraid that Lisa would look dowdy in contrast to Jane's expensive appearance. But from a distance one looked as smartly dressed as the other, and Peggy was glad.

It was only as they got closer that the difference became apparent in the mink collar on the suit Jane wore under her cashmere coat. Lisa's red suit was only a suit under her gray coat, and the red pillbox perched on her head was only a hat. But no one who glimpsed her face gave a second thought to her clothes. Even Peggy, knowing what Lisa looked like, caught her breath at the sight of the lovely, vibrant face framed by the cloud of softly waving black hair.

Lisa had stopped to put down her bag long enough to wave excitedly and say something to Jane, who nodded in reply. Then they came on with quickened steps, and in another moment she and Jane were close enough to really be seen and spoken to.

"Hi! What wonderful weather! How do you stand it?" Lisa laughed and, putting down her train case, threw her arms around Peggy. "This is like a dream! And it's all because of your wonderful aunt. I never thought I'd ever get to visit you and meet everyone you've been writing about."

Peggy hugged her in return and then turned to Jane and impulsively hugged her too. In the confused babble of voices, Mr. Andrews commanded, "Let's get inside, everybody, before these two exiles from warm weather freeze out here."

"Yes, please hurry!" Jane begged. "It's even colder than I remember its being."

They pushed in through the revolving door into the warmth of the building, and Mr. Andrews said, "You girls all sit down here while we get the rest of the bags. Give me your checks. Maybe we can get near the front of the line and not have to wait very long for your bags after they are brought in."

As her father and Bill walked away across the waiting room, Peggy realized that she hadn't introduced Lisa to anyone. Turning to her mother contritely, she said, "I'm sorry, I haven't even introduced you to each other. Although I guess you know who you are," she finished weakly, knowing the sentence was mixed up.

She looked at her mother anxiously and felt a wave

of relief at the warmth of her mother's voice as she spoke directly to Lisa, "I've heard so much about you, I don't think I need an introduction. We're all so glad you could come with Jane."

"Dad was certainly right," Peggy thought to herself, remembering he had said this was how her mother would be, and was glad.

Then Lisa, smiling back a little shyly, said, "Thank you so much. I would have known you too. You and Peggy are so much alike."

The words were a blow to Peggy and hit her with unexpected force. Was Lisa joking? Surely she must be! Was she like her mother? Did she have that perpetual fretting line around her mouth? Was she as quick to take offense at imagined slights? She had always thought of herself as being like her father in coloring and features and outlook on life.

In the brief interval of silence that followed Lisa's remark, Peggy searched her mother's face, looking for a resemblance. And then the moment of scrutiny passed as Mr. Andrews and Bill came toward them with the baggage. Mrs. Andrews frowned at Bill and shook her head imperceptibly at him as he clowned about the pretended weight of the luggage.

The events connected with Jane's last visit four years ago were hazy in Peggy's mind now, and she knew it was because she had deliberately put them out of her mind as something too unpleasant to think about. She did remember how much it had bothered her then that their car was old and their house seemed shabby. She could smile at herself about that now. It *would* be nice if they had the latest in everything, but she was adult enough now to realize that they didn't and couldn't, and let it go at that.

"I *am* different from Mother in that at least," she insisted silently on the way home. "That's what's bothered her so much about Aunt Emily's coming — the *things* she doesn't have."

And then they were nearing the house and Lisa was leaning forward to look out the window eagerly. "It's just the way I've pictured it, Peggy. The town, I mean, and your house. Everything is just the way I imagined it would be from what you have written. Where is your church from here?"

Peggy motioned. "About six blocks in that direction."

"And Ann's house? And Ellen's? And Alice's?"

"Do you want to swing around past those places?" Mr. Andrews looked back at them as he asked.

"No," his wife answered quickly. "Lunch is waiting, and the girls are probably tired and want to get warmed up. There'll be time later for that."

The thought of Ann gave Peggy a sinking feeling as she realized she still had to tell Lisa that she wouldn't be staying with them. She hoped Lisa wouldn't think it was funny that they weren't able to squeeze together enough to make room for her.

"I'll take you around this afternoon and introduce you to everybody," she promised.

And Jane said, "I'd like to meet everybody, too. I remember Ann, of course, from the time she and her folks visited you in California."

Mr. Andrews pulled into the driveway and stopped as close to the front door as possible and helped his wife out of the car, while Bill held the door for the girls.

"You get the bags out of the trunk, Bill, while I get the

front door unlocked." Mr. Andrews tossed Bill the car keys and hurried Lisa and Jane up to the porch, saying, "Come in quickly. Our weather really isn't so bad when you look out at it from inside a warm house."

Mrs. Andrews motioned Peggy back from the others and said in a low voice, "Perhaps we *could* make some arrangement for her to stay here with us after all. She doesn't seem like the kind to object to a little inconveniece. If Bill doesn't mind using his sleeping bag for a few nights, I think we could manage it."

"Could we really?" Peggy exclaimed in relief. "That would be wonderful! Fortunately, I haven't said anything to Lisa yet."

"The phone's ringing," Bill called back over his shoulder as he and his father stood by the door, waiting for the girls to go in.

"I'll get it," Peggy said and hurried in, not stopping to take off her coat. Grabbing the phone, she heard Ann's voice saying excitedly, "Peggy, I shouldn't be barging in on you when you're probably just back from the airport, but I couldn't *wait* to hear if she got here. Is she?"

"Yes, we just came in the door."

"Could I talk to her a minute? Just for a minute?"

"Yes, but —" Peggy looked over her shoulder. Lisa and Jane were standing by the hall closet while Mr. Andrews helped them with their coats. In a lower voice, she said into the phone, "Don't say anything to her, will you, Ann? I mean, about staying at your house. I — I haven't had a chance to tell her yet. And I think it would be better if I did."

"Okay, I won't say anything," Ann agreed but then she pleaded, "Don't back out now, Peggy. I'm really counting on having her here. I've got the extra bed in my room made up, so we're all set."

Peggy bit her lip. If only she hadn't said anything to Ann in the first place! Now it wouldn't be fair to change the plans. Aloud she said, "All right, I won't." Then she turned, "Lisa, Ann wants to talk to you."

With Lisa's eager voice and the sound of Ann's exclamations carrying clearly into the room, Peggy went out to the kitchen, where her mother was stirring a steaming kettle of cocoa, with a huge tray of sandwiches waiting on the kitchen table.

"Get out the cups, please, Peggy, and the salad from the refrigerator. We can eat in just a moment."

As she automatically did as she was told, Peggy said dolefully, "I guess we'd better go ahead with the plans to have Lisa sleep at Ann's. That was Ann on the phone, and she's counting on her coming."

"Probably," her mother replied absently, her mind already busy with more important problems. Then, seeing Peggy's disappointed face, she said, "I'm sorry. But it did seem so difficult at first to work it out. Perhaps this way it's just as well. It will give Jane more of a chance."

Peggy looked at her mother, not sure just what she meant. Then she thought back over the last hour and realized that Jane had scarcely said a word since their arrival and hardly anything had been said to her. Lisa had won everyone's attention so completely that Jane was merely a shadow. But then that was to be expected, she thought. There could only be one Lisa.

"When you do go over to Ann's house, be sure Lisa understands that she is to come here for Christmas day," Mrs. Andrews was reminding her. Peggy nodded. "And be sure Ann understands that, too, so they don't plan for her."

Peggy nodded again, but she couldn't help thinking that it wouldn't be nearly as good as having her actually staying with them the whole time.

She waited until they had finished lunch before saying, "Lisa, would you mind awfully having to stay with Ann? I hate for you to do it, but we only have three bedrooms and Ann is crazy to have you and —"

"Of course not," Lisa interrupted quickly with a warm smile. "If I had known sooner that I was coming and had had time to write, I would have asked you please not to go to any trouble for me. Naturally, I'd love to stay here, but it will be fun to be with Ann, too."

"We want you to feel free to come and go as you like," Mrs. Andrews urged. "And we want you for all of Christmas day."

"Why don't we three bunk together that one night?" Peggy suggested eagerly. "We wouldn't mind crowding together, would we, Jane?" she appealed, and Jane shook her head.

"But we'll have to be sure Ann understands that right from the beginning," she warned Lisa. "Once she gets you, she won't want to let you go, I'm afraid."

"I'll run you over when you're ready," Mr. Andrews offered. Peggy, with a quick look at the clock, said, "We'd better go as soon as we get the lunch dishes finished."

"You run along," Mrs. Andrews said. "Bill can help me with the dishes." She hesitated a minute and then said, "Peggy, if you want to invite Ann here for dinner this evening and bring Lisa back, you may."

Knowing how thoroughly her mother disliked impromptu invitations, even though her meals were always good enough to serve anyone who might come in unexpectedly, Peggy realized that the invitation was given with an effort to be gracious. She smiled at her mother appreciatively. "Thanks, Mother, but it will be fun just to be by ourselves for supper tonight."

Then she said hesitantly, "We — would like to go to the Christmas Eve service this evening. Remember? I told you about it last week."

Her mother nodded. "I remember," she said shortly, and that was all.

Lisa began to clear the table as they talked and Jane, after standing and watching a moment, helped. Peggy followed them out to the kitchen with a load of dishes in time to see Bill offer Jane an apron.

As Peggy watched in amazement, Bill said, "You can have your choice. Do you want to wash or wipe?"

Jane, looking helplessly at the sink and then at the stack of dishes, answered, "Maybe I'd better wipe. I've done that a few times, but I've never washed before."

Mrs. Andrews came out and, taking in the scene, said sharply, "Bill, I said *you* were to help. Jane is going with Peggy."

But Jane shook her head stubbornly. "I think I won't now. I can meet everybody later on," and no amount of urging would make her change her mind.

When Peggy stuck her head in the kitchen to say good-bye ten minutes later, Bill was washing the dishes while he explained in great detail and with many gestures, the various positions of his fingers in playing the trumpet. Jane was listening, apparently absorbed, as she slowly and awkwardly wiped the plates.

Peggy backed out, unseen, marveling as she always did over Bill's gift of charming anyone. Who else could make Jane willing to listen to something so boring!

Ann must have been watching out the window for

them, for as soon as Mr. Andrews stopped in front of the house, the door was flung open and Ann met them as they came up the walk. She and Lisa acted as though they'd known each other all their lives instead of having met only once before, and both began talking at once.

"Go on in and talk where it's warm," Mr. Andrews advised with a grin as he set Lisa's grips on the porch and went back to the car.

Mrs. Parker was waiting at the still-open front door and greeted Lisa warmly. "We're so glad to have you stay with us," she smiled. "Ann often needs a sister to help her hold her own against her brothers."

In the excitement of the next hour, Peggy managed to get the information that Larry was not home and wouldn't be until suppertime, the Parkers wanted Lisa for Christmas but would reluctantly give her up to Peggy, they were glad she was there in time for the Christmas Eve service, everyone was hoping she would be able to go on the retreat, and so on.

Peggy waited around as long as she could, hoping Larry might come in early, but he didn't, and she left at last reluctantly.

"See you tonight, Peg," Ann said and she nodded. To herself she added a fervent, "I hope!"

It all depended on her mother's feelings and moods. If Jane decided she didn't want to go, she knew her mother would think she should stay home too. "Maybe Bill could use some of his influence on Jane," she thought hopefully and walked home with quickened steps.

Running lightly up the front steps, she reached for the doorknob and felt it pulled at the same time from inside the house. The door opened, and to her surprise she found Ellen standing there.

"Hi! I didn't know you were here," Peggy exclaimed.

"I came over to see if your company had come. You and Lisa had just gone, so I invited myself to stay and talk to Jane. We've really been yakking," and Ellen grinned back over her shoulder at Jane. "At least I have been."

Peggy looked at Jane, thinking she had never seen her look so animated, and listened in amazement as Ellen went on, "Peggy's skates should fit you, Jane. Worm them out of her and go skating with me Saturday. Okay?"

Jane looked uneasy. "I'm not — not very good at skating," she finally said. Only Peggy, thinking back to her visit with Jane in California, knew what an effort it was for her to admit it.

But Ellen only laughed easily. "You'll learn. It's easy. We'll go kind of early before very many people get out on the ice. It's better then, smoother, you know, and easier to skate on. See you tonight!" With a wave of her hand she was gone, leaving Peggy staring after her.

She looked back at Jane. "Tonight?" she repeated.

Jane nodded. "She invited me to this service tonight and wanted me to sit with her. But — but I told her I'd rather sit with you and the rest of the family," she said shyly.

Peggy was delighted at the way this worked out. But once again she was caught up in an inexpressible longing. Everyone else was able to do something for the Lord. Only *she* was marking time!

10

Christmas Eve Service

THERE WAS just a hint of snow in the air as they got out of the car that evening and walked up the stairs to the entrance of the church. But the deep piles of snow that already weighted down the shrubs and low evergreen bushes along the steps and clung to the roof and steeple, made the church and its surroundings seem like a picture out of a book. The feeling of unreality was heightened as they stepped inside the darkened auditorium, lighted only by the soft glow of candles in the windows and in the candelabra across the front of the room.

The muted tone of the organ at first was only a whisper, barely audible over the rustlings and murmurs of those coming in. But gradually the music swelled into a quickening cadence of expectancy as well-loved Christmas carols reminded the listeners of the joy of the birth of Christ.

Peggy, listening, wished that her mother were there. Surely she would have been stirred by such music! For a little while she had been sure her mother would come since Jane obviously so much wanted to. But at the last moment she had shaken her head firmly.

"You go on," she said. "I'm too tired."

"You can rest there, Mom," Bill had urged. "You'll like it."

For a moment Peggy had thought her mother would give in, and then Bill had added, eagerly but thoughtlessly, "Besides, you've never been to one of these services."

That had done it and his mother had replied tartly, "And I'm not going to start now. Will you please go on and leave me in peace? I have things to get ready for tomorrow's dinner."

"I'm not going either," Mr. Andrews had said then. "You kids won't mind going alone, will you?"

"You don't need to stay home on my account," his wife had said sharply, and he answered, "No, I know that. But I would *rather* stay with you." His voice had been quiet and his look at her steady and, after a moment, Mrs. Andrews had turned away abruptly. Peggy was sure his offer wasn't appreciated but he didn't seem to mind.

So they had ridden over with Ellen and her mother, and now Peggy, looking along the row from where she sat beside Bill, could see Jane and Ellen sitting together on the other side of Mrs. Todd. How odd that they had hit it off so well.

When she and Bill were ushered to their seats, she had gotten a glimpse of Lisa, sitting with the Parkers, but couldn't see her now from where she sat. Alice was sitting by herself ahead of them, almost in the front row. She was to sing a solo in the service, and Peggy wondered if she should go up and sit with her, knowing how scared Ailce must be at the prospect of singing. Looking at the back of Alice's shining blond hair, Peggy felt a surge of remorse that she had reacted with such a savage feeling of jealousy at Larry's liking Alice. They had been friends too long for something like this to come between them. And yet — But Peggy made herself stop thinking.

Then, before she could get up, an usher brought Dan and his parents up to the row just behind Alice. After they were seated, Mrs. Schwartz leaned forward and said something to Alice, who nodded and slipped in with them, sitting on the end of the row next to Mr. Schwartz. Peggy saw the quick glance Dan gave in her direction before he stared straight ahead again. In that brief, intent look Peggy could read his longing. How well she could sympathize with him!

She noticed then that Mr. Schwartz was fidgety and looked around whenever someone was ushered down the aisle. Suddenly, as he looked back over his shoulder just as Mr. Parker came onto the platform, she heard him give a low, sudden exclamation under his breath. He whispered something to Alice who nodded and moved slightly to let him crowd past her into the aisle.

As Peggy watched, she could feel her mouth drop open in amazement as Mr. Verbeck, stopping to shake Mr. Schwartz' outstretched hand, was urged into the row next to Mrs. Schwartz. She couldn't help exchanging amazed looks with Ellen. Who would ever have expected to see Mr. Verbeck in church?

How did he ever get to know Dan's folks, she wondered. And who had invited him to church? And, most amazing of all, what ever had made him willing to come?

At first Peggy couldn't take her eyes or mind off Mr. Verbeck as she speculated over the reason for his being there. But gradually she was caught up in the mood and atmosphere of the service. Only once did her attention wander, and that was when Alice first stood up to sing. She found herself clenching her fists as she had done at other times in the past when Alice had been cornered into singing and Peggy had agonized with her until the ordeal was over. But tonight, though Peggy could see that her hands trembled as she held the sheet of music, her voice was relaxed and there was an assurance about her that Peggy had never seen before.

Mr. Verbeck was listening intently, she noticed, and then she turned her own attention to the message of the song. The words were simple, the melody unadorned. The simplicity of the song and the depth of sincerity in Alice's voice carried the message with poignant force to Peggy, sensitive as she was just then to the urgency of hearing God speak to her personally, individually.

She puzzled over the way the chorus sang itself in her mind long after Alice had sat down, and on through the prayer and into Mr. Parker's message.

> O come to my heart, Lord Jesus
> There is room in my heart for Thee.

Why did it repeat itself over and over again? She had long ago asked Him in. Was it, she wondered, the last part of the refrain that was bothering her? Did He really have room?

She thought back over the last few months with its same routine and — she admitted it with shame — its same failures. She had learned in the past years through hard experiences, to really pray for others and to really trust God for someone's salvation. She had learned the futility of trying to go through a day without a quiet time with the Lord.

"Then why?" she found herself asking with a feeling of desperation. "Why should a little thing like dating become so important?" She knew she ought not to let it consume all her thinking. Yet it had done just that. She could pray about other things but not about this. It had blinded her so that she couldn't even see anybody else's need.

Alice had been sensitive to Mr. Verbeck and had spoken to him. Peggy was sure that somehow Alice was responsible for his being in the service tonight. And Ellen, direct, practical, tactless Ellen, had gotten through to Jane. While she, who so longed to be used, was useless. And the worst part of it was that it was her own fault.

Through the haze that surrounded her, as she sat looking up at the pulpit with the sense that there was something in this moment that only needed to be taken and it would be important for all her life, Mr. Parker's quiet, intense voice reached her and his words stung her with the answer.

"The meaning of this moment of time needs to be rekindled every day in your experience of living for Christ. It isn't enough only to ask Him in, though that is all you need to do for salvation. But for earnest, daily, meaningful living, you must surrender every day to Him. You must give Him room to work out His will in you."

There was more, but that was enough for Peggy just then, and she knew it was her answer. She didn't have to continue with this feeling of defeat. There could be a new beginning for her even now. She could have the fire of God constantly burning with power within her if only she would be willing to have it.

Peggy stood with the rest of the congregation in the stillness of the candlelit moment and prayed her own prayer of surrender as Mr. Parker gave the benediction.

As she raised her head, she saw Mr. Schwartz turn to Mr. Verbeck immediately with a wordless smile and a firm handshake, and then Mr. Verbeck leaned across him to say to Alice, "You surprise me constantly with your talents."

Alice flushed, but before she could answer, Mr. Schwartz said earnestly, "She does not just believe what she sings. Nein, she lifs it also." In his earnestness his accent had crept in, though Peggy knew how hard he tried to control it for Dan's sake.

Then Mr. Verbeck turned and, seeing Peggy, raised his eyebrows. "You come here too?" he asked.

She nodded, and his eyes went on to take in Ellen and then Bob and others whom he had in class. Then he nodded in Alice's direction. "But only this one speaks of it." His voice made it a flat statement, but Peggy noticed again the slight accent that was apparent only when he was excited.

There was an awkward moment of silence, and then Mrs. Schwartz said, "We are so glad that she spoke to us of you. It is not good to be always all alone."

She appealed around to the others. "He is living in our town for five years, two blocks from us, and we do not know of it. And he has no one, no family. They are all gone." Her face held indescribable sadness. "And then Alice told us. She said he needed help. *Needed,*" she repeated. "To need something and have no one to help — it is bad."

"But now, now we think he will find it." Mr. Schwartz broke the spell as he put his hand on the other man's arm and shook it affectionately while he looked at him questioningly.

Peggy, along with the others, was like a statue, mutely uncomfortable at this public display of affection and terribly afraid Mr. Verbeck would resent it and leave. But instead he nodded slowly, gripping his hat so tightly that his knuckles were white. "I — I think — at last there is room," he said simply.

"Come. We go and talk to our pastor. He will help." And Mr. Schwartz led him down the aisle while the others watched in silence and Peggy tried to swallow past the huge lump in her throat.

No one seemed inclined to talk as they left the church and during the brief ride home, and Peggy was glad. But she made herself take part in the family conversation when they found their parents in the living room before the lighted tree. There was only one reference to the service and that was when Peggy, in response to her father's question, mentioned that Alice had sung.

"Boy, is Dan ever gone on her!" Bill exclaimed. "I was sitting where I could see his face while she was singing, and he couldn't pry his eyes loose."

Peggy only nodded. She wasn't ready tonight, yet, to grapple with the practical reality of the commitment she had just made. She knew she would have to — sometime.

Later, as they were getting ready for bed, Jane asked, "Dan? Is that the dark boy who sat in front of us?"

"Yes."

"They do seem different. Alice and he, I mean. He looks as though he's only thinking of himself all the time and she looks — oh, I don't know — as though she'd like to be helping somebody. I just *love* her voice."

"She wasn't always like that though. Let me tell you what happened to her." And Peggy told her all the events of the past summer, ending regretfully, "You really can't tell just by looking at her how much she has changed. I wish I were as different since I've been a Christian as she is." Her voice was wistful, and she hardly realized that she had said the thought aloud until, catching sight of the embarrassed look on Jane's face, she turned abruptly and settled herself on the bed, tucking a pillow behind her.

She smiled across at Jane and said, "Let's talk, shall we? If you're not sleepy, that is."

"I don't think I can sleep all night," Jane answered, and a slow smile warmed her face and took away the wary expression from her eyes. Peggy realized with a shock how much Jane had changed in appearance in the last two years and felt as though she were looking at a carbon copy of herself as a freshman. Except that Jane had more self-confidence than she had ever had!

"It doesn't seem possible that you only got here this noon!" Peggy exclaimed. "It seems like ages ago! Tell me all about yourself and everyone I know." She caught herself just in time to keep from asking about Janet. That could present a problem, and she didn't want any problems with Jane, not during this visit. Tonight she wanted to be sure they were on a warm, friendly basis. This week could mean a lot in Jane's life.

Peggy listened as Jane talked, telling about Sally, Miss Murphy, Mrs. Tremont, and others whom Peggy remembered. Her voice took on a softer tone as she said, "Uncle Walter wanted so much to come. It was his idea in the first place, and after all the talking he had to do to convince Aunt Emily, I felt awful that he couldn't come."

"I did, too. But anyway you did. And Lisa."

"I'm glad she did. I wasn't crazy about the idea of coming alone. She's nice," Jane said reflectively. "But she's like — I don't know. She's like an older sister. I mean, *really* older, you know? You never think of her as being someone you can — well — goof off with. I don't know how to explain it."

"I think I know what you mean."

"Uncle Walter said once he didn't see how anyone who was so beautiful could be so serious-minded."

"That really does describe her," Peggy agreed. "Probably that's because she's always had a lot of responsibility. She had to sort of grow up when she was young."

"I don't think she dates anybody very much. I asked her once if she went out a lot, and she said she didn't have time."

This was something Peggy had been curious about, for Lisa had never mentioned dating anyone. She couldn't imagine anyone as beautiful as Lisa not being swamped with dates. "Maybe I'm not the only one after all," she thought with a wry smile.

Jane yawned widely then. "I guess I'm sleepier than I thought."

"We'd better get to bed, I guess," Peggy said reluctantly. She hated to stop, since this was almost the first real, sisterly, friendly talk like this they had ever had. Then she asked, "Do you mind if I read aloud from my Bible?"

"No, go ahead." And Jane dug out her file and did her nails while Peggy read the ninety-first Psalm.

She hesitated momentarily when she got down to the fifteenth verse. "He shall call upon me, and I will answer him . . ." Mr. Parker had once said, she remembered, that this verse should be read with the words in the ninth verse, and she glanced back at them. "Because thou hast made the Lord, which is my refuge, even the most High, thy habitation."

As she prayed aloud, briefly, she thought of her prayer of surrender just a short time before and added now a silent, heartfelt plea that she might always remember that the Lord was her refuge.

Later, out of the dark, Jane said, "I like Ellen."

"Umhmm, she's fun to be around," Peggy answered,

realizing suddenly that Jane and Ellen were very much alike in the way they said and did things.

"She — uh — she asked if I would go on this retreat next week."

Peggy waited, hardly daring to hope and Jane went on, "She wants me to learn how to skate."

"She should be good at teaching it because she's sure good at it herself. I think I'll come along, too." It seemed to Peggy though, as she answered, that there was more Jane wanted to say.

And, after a moment, her voice came again, softer than Peggy had ever remembered hearing it, and a little shyly. "Ellen said that there are other things I need to learn about too. Like — being saved. Lisa has explained a lot to me. And, of course, Uncle Walter is — well, so different since — since he became a Christian. Though he isn't as good at explaining things to me as he is to his friends. But anyway, Ellen says it's awfully important." Jane stopped and then finished, "It sounds like fun. I think I'll go."

Peggy let out a long, quiet breath of relief and almost said out loud, "Thank You! Thank You!"

11

A Prayer Answered

CHRISTMAS DAY was a little warmer, with a bright sun that gave a sparkling glitter to the snow and reflected on the icy branches of the trees so that they looked like shining jeweled swords.

Jane, looking out the window after a late, leisurely breakfast, said wonderingly, "I never knew snow could look so pretty."

"There's something about this kind of weather that makes you feel as though you could lick the world," Bill agreed.

His father, surveying him as he stretched out in an easy chair practically on the end of his spine, replied dryly, "Not from that position, you won't. Let's see you lick some of the snow from the sidewalk — and driveway."

"Right now?" Bill asked in anguished tones.

"Right now!"

"We're not going anyplace, are we? That we need the driveway cleared, I mean?" he asked.

"We're going to get Lisa pretty soon," Peggy answered.

"Well, look, if that's all, I'll walk over and get her. Or, better yet, we can ask Larry to bring her over."

"Bill, stop arguing," Mrs. Andrews said tartly. "You might just as well get the job done, since you have to do it sooner or later."

"Later is better than sooner." Bill grinned at her as

he reluctantly got to his feet. "I thought if I waited until nearer dinner, I'd work up a better appetite."

They had all decided it would be best to wait until after dinner to open the gifts so that Lisa could be in on it too. Peggy was glad her mother had planned a menu that didn't require a lot of last-minute preparation. She had helped fix a fruit salad while Jane awkwardly peeled potatoes.

Now Peggy, arranging the centerpiece for the table with tall, slender red candles and white crysanthymums, stepped back to eye it with a critical frown.

"It doesn't look just right somehow," Bill said from behind her shoulder and she retorted, "Well, thanks!" knowing, though, that he was right.

Mrs. Andrews came in when she heard him and with swift fingers deftly rearranged it just enough for Peggy to exclaim, "There! That's perfect!" Then she asked enviously, "How do you do it?"

Her mother shrugged off the compliment with its obvious admiration. "My one gift," she retorted.

"Yeah? That's what you think," Bill said as he started to the basement for the shovel. "I think your cooking is your best gift."

"You would!" Peggy said, but Mrs. Andrews said sharply, "That's no gift. I learned that through hard experience." Peggy thought, silently, that another gift was her mother's ability to raise, with just a few words, the specter of unpleasant memories, as she had done now.

The ringing of the doorbell was a welcome interruption, and Peggy hurried to answer exclaiming, "I'll bet that's Lisa and she had to plow up to the door through all the snow Bill was supposed to have shoveled off by this time!"

"I'm on my way," he called back as he disappeared through the back door.

It was Lisa, and Ann and Larry were with her and Peggy felt her heart pound and her breath catch as usual at the sight of his slow, warming grin.

"Hi," she said. "Come on in, everybody."

"We can't, Peg," Ann answered. "We're supposed to pick up some people for dinner, and it's almost time to get them."

"I could just as well have walked up to the door from the car myself," Lisa was protesting to them, laughingly.

"But we both came along to make sure you remembered she was coming back to us tomorrow," Ann broke in.

"We've got an unfinished ping-pong game to work out and need her back as Jim's partner," Larry added, putting Lisa's train case down just inside the door.

Peggy hadn't looked directly at him after the first quick glance and didn't now until he turned to go down the steps, piloting Ann along the narrow path Bill was hastily cleaning for them.

"We've been having so much fun!" Lisa exclaimed as she slipped out of her red coat and hung it in the closet. Her eyes were so sparkling, Peggy didn't think even Uncle Walter could call her serious-minded if he could see her now. This vacation was bringing out a part of her personality Peggy had never seen, and it seemed her beauty was intensified.

The dinner was, as usual, excellently prepared and beautifully served. Peggy was sure only her mother could manage to serve such a meal so easily without extra help. She couldn't remember ever having seen her mother enter as completely into the conversation as she did at the dinner table that day. She was so warm and gracious toward

Lisa that Peggy was almost ready to believe she had imagined that her mother had so strongly objected to her coming with Jane.

Mrs. Andrews had decided to do the dishes of the main course right after dinner and then have dessert and coffee and nuts in the living room before the long-deferred opening of gifts.

"Can you imagine us waiting this long when we were kids?" Peggy asked as she helped carry in the dessert and put it on the individual trays Bill had already set out.

"I remember sneaking down one night and opening everything that had my name on it," he returned with a grin.

"Yes, and you opened some of mine, too, 'by mistake' you said," Peggy reminded him.

"These are too pretty to unwrap," Lisa said, admiring the packages. "I'm glad I can just sit back and watch the rest of you, since we had Christmas at home before I left."

"You won't get off that easily," Mr. Andrews said. "I saw your name on a couple of those packages. Look at that tall, skinny one there."

"Dad!" Peggy protested. "Be careful or she'll guess!"

Since she had already mailed Lisa's gift to her home, Peggy had dashed downtown Thursday morning, before they went to the airport, to pick up a bottle of perfume just to have something under the tree for her.

A large box had come in the mail several weeks ago from Aunt Emily, and the packages it contained had been added to those already wrapped and waiting to be opened. Her gifts, expensive, well chosen, and beautifully wrapped, were a reminder to Peggy of what money could do, and she looked apprehensively at her mother as she opened her gift and held it up. It was a very lovely necklace. But, except for a brief murmur of appreciation as she held it up for a moment against her neck, there was no change in her manner or expression.

It was Lisa who later gathered up the wrapping paper and folded it neatly with the ribbons while Mrs. Andrews drew the drapes behind the softly glowing tree.

"Home seems so far away," Lisa said into the silence. Her voice was dreamy and yet held a hint of sadness.

"And yet it isn't either," Jane spoke up and once again the tone of her voice startled Peggy with its reminder of Ellen.

"I mean, well, you know — everyone is having a Christmas tree and stuff, aren't they?" Jane appealed around the circle.

"Everyone has the same basic Christmas observances, you mean?" her father asked, and Jane nodded.

"But not everyone thinks of it mainly as the birthday of the Lord Jesus," Lisa said softly. "And, of course, it has no meaning at all apart from Him."

In the silence that followed, Peggy remembered the sentence out of Myling's latest letter to Miss Method.

"Christmas?" she had written. "What is that for me to be happy about? I shall have my same bowl of rice — no, you are right. Christmas *is* a time to be happy, for I shall have a small piece of fish with the rice."

The words and their meaning had been biting and had come through to the girls in spite of the halting way Myling expressed herself in English. Peggy had finally volunteered to write the next letter and wished now she hadn't, for she hadn't the least idea what to say to her. No matter what anyone wrote, Myling seemed to take it the wrong way.

But now, as she sat on the floor and leaned back against

the side of the chair in which Lisa was sitting, she felt too contented to analyze anyone's feelings or probe into anyone's problems. She was dreamily aware that her father had gotten up quietly to turn on the record player, and she listened to the lovely Christmas music that poured over the room. The minutes melted into one another, as each one sat engrossed in his own private thoughts.

Then Peggy, a million miles away, was jerked back to the present as she happened to glance at her mother and saw the expression on her face as she sat looking at Jane. There was a stark, hungering look of love that almost squeezed Peggy's heart with its intensity. It was wiped out instantly as Mrs. Andrews seemed to realize that someone was looking at her. She raised her head to look back at Peggy and in the second or two that they stared at each other, Peggy felt again, as she had last summer, that she didn't really know her mother. She sensed that there must be unimagined depths of longings and dreams that had never been realized in her mother's life.

Her father's words came back again with new meaning: "She lost everything and has never gotten it back." It was Jane that her mother missed and wanted. It was Jane who was the center of her mother's thinking. In the brief look she and her mother exchanged, Peggy could read it as clearly as though the words had been spoken aloud.

Then the spell was broken as Mrs. Andrews rose abruptly and switched on a table lamp.

"I hope you can all eat turkey sandwiches, because we've got lots of it to use up," she said. The practicality of her voice brought them all back to the reality of the present as they blinked their eyes in the sudden brighter light.

Only Peggy didn't join in Bill's, "Who couldn't eat

turkey sandwiches any day!" And Lisa's, "Let me help." And Jane's, "I'll eat the turkey without the sandwich."

Peggy purposely sat still while the others got up. After that revealing glimpse into her mother's secret heart, she felt as though she couldn't face her, or anyone else, just yet. But her father reached down a hand for her and she took it reluctantly and let him help her up. He held her back and shielded her from the rest of the family.

"Why don't you talk to her about it?" he asked quietly.

"You saw too?" she asked. Suddenly she felt her lips tremble, and she looked away from his sympathetic face.

He nodded. "It isn't as bad as you think. It's not as though you and Bill are not loved equally as well. But Jane represents —" He stopped and looked at her, apparently unable to put it into words. Peggy knew what he was trying to say, but deliberately refused to understand. She turned away from him to help prepare the sandwiches.

As she went through the rest of the evening, answering questions when asked and making the proper responses to all that was said to her, she felt almost as if someone else were speaking through her.

But as she thought about it, she gradually realized that what her father had said was true. Jane did seem special to her mother because she had had to give her up when she was just a baby. How awful that must have been, she thought compassionately. Even her own problem didn't loom as large in proportion.

"And, of course," she reminded herself, "I still can hope that mine will work out the way I want it to." So she shrugged off her serious thoughts and was as giggly as Lisa and Jane when Bill brought his mattress into her room and dumped it on the floor.

"This is very comfortable," she answered in reply to

their protests that one of them should sleep on the floor. "This isn't the floor anyway. If I do roll off, it will get me in practice for skating tomorrow. I haven't been skating at all this year yet, and I'm going to have to learn all over."

"What about me?" Lisa asked. "I haven't been ever. I'm the one who will fall."

"Hey, are you going tomorrow, too?" Jane asked, and Lisa said, "Yes, Ann thinks I haven't lived until I've skated, so she persuaded me to go. She said she could borrow skates from someone for me."

"Let's all go together then," Jane exclaimed enthusiastically, and Peggy agreed, wondering if she should call Alice and invite her. "Though probably Larry already has," her heart reminded her with a momentary twinge of envy.

As they talked, Peggy's mind was taken from the tangled thoughts of the afternoon by the difference that kept showing up in Lisa. It wasn't terribly obvious, but there was a subtle change in her, an exuberance that Peggy had never noticed before. She didn't know what had caused it, but was glad for Lisa's sake that she was having such a good time.

It was Jane who woke them up the next morning when her hairbrush fell with a clatter to the dresser and then bounced off onto the floor.

"Oh, I'm sorry!" she exclaimed. "I thought I was going to be so quiet and sneak out without waking you."

"What are you doing up so early?" Peggy yawned and then, as her eyes focused on the clock, she exclaimed, "How did it get that late? It's almost nine-thirty!"

Lisa sat up, startled, and exclaimed, "Nine-thirty! I'd better get dressed fast!"

Then as Peggy really looked at Jane and saw that she was dressed, she asked, "Are you going already?"

"Yes, Ellen is coming in about ten minutes. We're going to practice before the rest of you get there."

"Okay, see you there." And Peggy flopped back to doze a few minutes more while Lisa was showering.

After a quick breakfast, Lisa had gone upstairs again to finish getting ready, and Peggy had stopped for a minute in the living room, when the phone rang.

"Hi, Peg!" Ann's voice came over breathlessly. "Want to go skating?"

"Yeah, I thought I would. I was going with Jane and Ellen, but they went ahead by themselves. Are you going now?"

"In just a few minutes. I — I wondered, should Bob stop by for you after he picks me up? Since Jane and Ellen have gone, I mean?"

"Well, thanks, but — You're not forgetting Lisa, are you?" Peggy teased.

Ann hesitated and then said, "No, but —" It seemed as though the words were being dragged out of her and Peggy frowned over it, wondering what she was finding so hard to say.

"But what?" she asked and then, as the doorbell rang and no one else seemed to be going to answer it, she said, "Wait a minute, Ann, don't hang up. Someone's at the door. Be right back."

She put the receiver down, crossed to the door, and opened it.

"Well, hi," she said, and her heart turned over as she looked up at Larry.

"Hi, Peg. Is — is — is Lisa here?"

Then, as Peggy stared at him, Larry's eyes went to someone behind her and lit up. Peggy had her answer — the answer she had been afraid to pray for. It was no. It wasn't even Alice that he liked. It was to be Larry and Lisa.

Anyone could see that from the way they looked at one another. And then Lisa said shyly and with that glow she'd had ever since coming from their house yesterday, "Just a minute. I'm almost ready."

Peggy stood in the open doorway, not even feeling the cold, and glad Lisa was all ready to put on her coat. She didn't think she could keep the false smile pasted on her lips indefinitely. Her face ached with the effort of keeping it composed and smiling as Lisa said, "We'll see you there, Peggy, in a little while." And Larry said, "I think Ann is going to call and offer you a ride."

Peggy nodded and closed the door behind them, leaning her forehead against it numbly. Then, belatedly, she remembered that Ann was still waiting on the phone.

Swallowing hard, she crossed to it and picked up the receiver.

"Ann? Sorry to keep you waiting." And then her throat closed in and she couldn't say anything more.

"They — they've gone? I mean, he came?" Ann's voice was anxious and concerned and understanding — and regretful. Dimly Peggy realized that Ann knew how she felt about Larry, and she wondered how many others had known what she thought she had kept hidden.

Suddenly she couldn't stand the thought of going with them and seeing them together. Ann and Bob would be paired off and Alice and Dan, and now Lisa and — Even Bill would be hanging around Candy as though she had never been on skates before.

"I'm not going," she said with loud, abrupt decision, forgetting even that she was still talking into the phone.

There was silence for a moment, and then Ann said in a troubled voice, "Well, okay, Peggy, if you're sure —"

"Sure of what?" Peggy snapped, suddenly furious at everyone and everything.

"Sure that's the best way to handle it."

"There's nothing to handle," she answered stiffly. And then, "Look, I've got to hang up. I'll see you."

She put the phone down slowly and stood looking at it, she didn't know how long, her thoughts muddled. She felt completely lost and as though she had been cheated out of something.

Then she was aware that her mother had come into the living room with the silver tray and teapot, ordinarily used only for guests, and with two of the fragile cups and saucers that had been treasured wedding gifts.

Avoiding looking directly at Peggy, she said, "Have a cup of tea with me, dear. I feel like being lazy today after all of yesterday's activity."

"Oh, I — I don't think —" Peggy began, squeezing the words out in a tight voice. But her mother went on calmly pouring the tea and measuring out lemon and sugar with a practiced hand.

She held out a cup, and Peggy took it blindly and sat down in a chair across from her mother and slightly out of range of her vision. She shook her head at the silver tray of thinly sliced fruit cake, but her mother said, "Try it. Sometimes these recipes you come across in the paper don't amount to anything. But now and then you find a real treasure. This is one."

Peggy took a slice and laid it beside her cup, which she didn't dare pick up for fear her unsteady hand would

make it spill. Her heart cried out, "How can Mother talk
about such unimportant things when I've just lost what
I most wanted?"

Mrs. Andrews sipped her tea appreciatively before she
said companionably, "There's nothing like a cup of hot
tea when you think the world and everything you want
is lost forever. It seems to bring things back into focus
somehow."

Peggy stared down at the saucer held tight between her
hands and listened as her mother went on, "None of us are
immune from problems. There was a time when I thought
I had them all, and I thought each one was larger than
those anyone else had. The trouble was I never learned
to cope with them. I never had anything — or anyone —
to really help."

"Except a cup of tea!" Peggy raised her head and
looked at her mother and then was ashamed of the bitterness and anger in her voice, for her mother looked directly
back at her and answered, "You see, Peggy, when I gave
my baby — Jane — up for her good and for what seemed
best for you and Bill, it was a symbol of defeat. Emily
had always had everything her way, and now she had my
baby. It has colored all my thinking and living since then."

She hesitated, as though what was coming was even
harder to say. Then she said slowly, "I didn't know anything about God. I didn't know there was anyone who
made heartaches bearable." She stopped and looked directly at Peggy, compelling her to meet her gaze, and
then asked, "Do you?"

The question was like a knife cutting away the pretense
Peggy knew she had thrown around herself through these
months. She had refused to trust God to answer her
prayer in this thing, wanting only her own way in it. Even

her prayer last night had had a reservation, she knew now, for although she had prayed for God's will to be done, she had resented the answer when it came.

Her mother came across to her and said softly, "You think I haven't known what has been bothering you lately? I have. And it's something that time works out. When the right person comes along, you'll know it. In the meantime, just take things as they come. Don't try to force things to work the way you want them to. Sometimes that isn't best. I know."

And then the tears came flooding down Peggy's cheeks as she put down her cup and buried her head against her mother as she hadn't done for long years. The tears were for her mother and the sadness that had been her companion for so long. And they were for herself that she could have been so selfish. And, in this moment of closeness, Peggy's surrender became real as she whispered, "Yes, I do know the only One who makes heartaches bearable."

And now her prayer was to show Him to her mother also.